"Mama! You're Squishing Me!"

M   b   r
s
su   d
wedding band stood out starkly on one ~~~~ ~~~r.

A ring he himself had slipped on.

His gaze shot back to her pale face, to the stark panic she couldn't disguise.

And suddenly it all fit.

The ring, her distress, the little boy's bright blue eyes and familiar grin…

Familiar because it was the spitting image of his, seen captured in photos and reflected in mirrors for his entire thirty-four years.

Dear Reader,

Cowboys and cops...sexy men with a swagger...just the kind of guys to make your head turn. *That's* what we've got for you this month in Silhouette Desire.

The romance begins when Taggart Jones meets his match in Anne McAllister's wonderful MAN OF THE MONTH, *The Cowboy and the Kid*. This is the latest in her captivating CODE OF THE WEST miniseries. And the fun continues with Mitch Harper in *A Gift for Baby*, the next book in Raye Morgan's THE BABY SHOWER series.

Cindy Gerard has created a dynamic hero in the *very* masculine form of J. D. Hazzard in *The Bride Wore Blue*, book #1 in the NORTHERN LIGHTS BRIDES series. And if rugged rascals are your favorite, don't miss Jake Spencer in Dixie Browning's *The Baby Notion*, which is book #1 of DADDY KNOWS LAST, Silhouette's new cross-line continuity. (Next month, look for Helen R. Myers's *Baby in a Basket* as DADDY KNOWS LAST continues in Silhouette Romance!)

Gavin Cantrell is sure to weaken your knees in *Gavin's Child* by Caroline Cross, part of the delightful BACHELORS AND BABIES promotion. And Jackie Merritt—along with hero Duke Sheridan—kicks off her MADE IN MONTANA series with *Montana Fever*.

Heroes to fall in love with—and love scenes that will make your toes curl. That's what Silhouette Desire is all about. Until next month—enjoy!

All the best,

Lucia Macro

Senior Editor

Please address questions and book requests to:
Silhouette Reader Service
U.S.: 3010 Walden Ave., P.O. Box 1325, Buffalo, NY 14269
Canadian: P.O. Box 609, Fort Erie, Ont. L2A 5X3

CAROLINE CROSS
CROSS
GAVIN'S CHILD

SILHOUETTE *Desire*®
Published by Silhouette Books
America's Publisher of Contemporary Romance

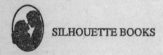

SILHOUETTE BOOKS

ISBN 0-373-76013-2

GAVIN'S CHILD

Printed in U.S.A.

CAROLINE CROSS

grew up in eastern Washington State, where she acquired a love of books and horses, long summer days and wide-open spaces. Although she was an inveterate reader, it wasn't until after the birth of her second child that she discovered the magic of contemporary romance fiction. Fascinated by the opportunity to write about what interests her most—people, and why they behave as they do—she began her first book and has been writing ever since. She now lives outside Seattle with her husband, two daughters and an ever-expanding collection of pets.

To Pat Teal—savvy friend and wise counselor

And to Melinda, Susan and Sandi—three of the brightest, nicest—*most irreverent*—friends anyone could have. Thanks guys.

Prologue

Someone was watching him.

Gavin Cantrell paused as he reached for the six-pack of beer. A prickle of primitive awareness crept up his broad, powerful back. It was so strong that he had to fight an uneasy urge to roll his shoulders.

Instead, he stood as still as a statue and tried to pinpoint the source of the feeling. First he narrowed his eyes against the artificial brightness of the fluorescent lights overhead. Next he blocked out the insistent voice on the grocery store's PA system, which was requesting that shoppers be on the lookout for a missing toddler.

He eased back, two hundred and ten pounds of muscled aggression, and took a long look around.

The aisle was deserted.

Well, hell. There's nobody here but you, Rambo.

The tension slowly drained out of him, and a wash of heat worked its way up his neck. He shook his head. How much longer was it going to take for the overactive defense mechanisms he'd learned at Colson to fade? How long before he stopped seeing enemies in every shadow and threats around every bend? Another month? A year? Ten?

He raked a hand through his dark hair and let loose a sigh of disgust. All right, so he'd overreacted. It was no big deal. He was just tired—and hot, sweaty and hungry after thirteen hours working full-out on the Ebersoles' new house. His foot ached from the beam an apprentice carpenter had inadvertently dropped on it. And his shoulders stung because he'd foolishly worked bare-chested under the hot June sun.

All he needed was a cold drink, a long shower and a hot meal, then he'd feel more like himself.

None of which he was likely to get standing around here, he reminded himself. Any more than the twenty-mile drive north to the furnished room he called home was going to get shorter. Sighing, he reached once more for the beer—only to be brought up short as the sensation of being watched skated along his spine again.

Disgusted, he started to grab the six-pack anyway, determined not to be drawn into whatever crude game his psyche was playing. Suddenly a slight movement at the end of the aisle caught his eye. He dropped his hand—vaguely aware that the voice on the PA system was now droning something about blue rompers and red sneakers—and waited.

Ten seconds passed. Then twenty. He'd just about decided he really was imagining things when a child peeked around the corner. The little boy, barely bigger than a minute, had an angel's face beneath a mop of silky, moonbeam-colored hair.

For a span of seconds he watched Gavin warily out of large, mischievous blue eyes, the color as clear and deep as Gavin's own. And then he hooked his thumbs behind his ears, made a comically ferocious face and waggled his fingers.

The last of the tension seeped out of Gavin's big frame. *I'll be damned.* He looked around, confident that any second now some chiding mama or disgruntled sibling would appear and put an end to the kid's horseplay.

And then he glanced down and registered the crimson color of the boy's itty-bitty sneakers.

Well, *hell.* The good news, obviously, was that the PA system's missing toddler hadn't been abducted.

The bad news was that only he and the kid appeared to know it.

He considered his options. The most logical course of action would be to grab the little fugitive and haul him up to the manager's counter. Yet as big as Gavin was—and, at the moment, as dirty and disheveled—such a move would probably scare the starch right out of the little guy. Gavin didn't want any trouble—particularly not the sort he'd get if the kid kicked up a fuss at being manhandled and somebody got the wrong idea.

Gavin's expression darkened. He knew all about wrong ideas. He should; he'd spent thirty-four months at the state correctional facility at Colson, courtesy of the State of Colorado, because the Pueblo County prosecutor had had one about him.

He could just imagine what the reaction would be in this situation if somebody found out he was an ex-con. Not to mention what might happen to his current freedom if he were accused of child abduction.

The thought of being locked up again made his stomach roll.

If he had a brain in his head, he would grab the beer and get the hell out of here. Except...what if the kid wandered off and ran into real trouble? Even though it wasn't Gavin's concern, and even though it'd serve whoever *was* accountable right to get a royal fright, he couldn't very well let the kid pay the price for some adult's lack of responsibility.

Besides, he thought gruffly, slanting the child an exasperated glance, he really was a cute little guy....

He sighed as a possible solution struck him. It wasn't much, and, God knew, just the idea made him feel like four kinds of fool.

On the other hand, if it kept the kid from wandering off until some good, respectable, law-abiding citizen showed up to rescue him, he supposed it was worth a try.

Which wasn't a hell of a lot of comfort for how ridiculous he felt as he turned his head and stuck out his tongue.

The child's hands stilled. His eyes opened wide with surprise. Then he hastily ducked back around the corner.

Gavin slammed his mouth shut, nearly swallowing his tongue. Terrific. He'd scared the kid off and now—

The boy popped back around the corner. A devilish gleam in his bright blue eyes, he screwed up his little face in concentration and stuck out his tongue.

Relief flooded Gavin. He matched the boy's action—and crossed his eyes, as well.

Again, the child looked startled. Then his entire face lit up in a shy, lopsided grin, and he laughed.

The high, bright sound was irresistible. So was that smile. Yet Gavin frowned, swept by a sudden, inexplicable sense of recognition. Puzzled, he studied the boy, taking in the sturdy little body, the pink and cream complexion, the winged brows, the button nose, the rosebud mouth. The kid was a charmer, no doubt about it, but Gavin was sure he'd never seen him before. Still, there was something about that smile, about the way it crooked up at one corner that—

"Sam!"

The frantic feminine voice at his back blew his train of thought right off the rails. In the next instant a woman rushed past, leaving the faint scent of white lilacs in her path.

Gavin watched, transfixed, as she slid to her knees and scooped the child into her slender arms.

"Oh, Sam!" She gathered the toddler close and buried her face in the crook of his neck. Her hair, the same thick, silver gilt as the child's, was caught up in a high ponytail that spilled down her back like a cascade of silk. It exposed the creamy, vulnerable curve of her nape and the slim, delicate line of her back. "You scared me half to death, sweetie." A tremor went through her as she fought for composure. "You know you're not to ever, *ever* go where I can't see you. And—" she lifted her head, setting the child away just enough so they could see each other "—you're not supposed to talk to strangers. Remember?"

Eyes huge, the little boy nodded. "'Kay."

"Good." She immediately gave him another fierce hug, then turned her head slightly, for the first time acknowledging Gavin's presence. "I'm sorry if he was bothering you," she said, struggling a little as she got her legs beneath her and hefted the child up. "I only looked away for a moment, and the next thing I knew, I couldn't find him. He's so fast, like quicksilver—" She stopped and swallowed. Hard. "I'm sorry. I don't know what I'd do if anything happened to him...."

Gavin knew what she'd look like before she turned. He knew her nose would be small and straight, her cheekbones elegant, her mouth lush, her eyes big, dark and mysterious. He knew she would have the sort of cool, quiet beauty that made a man burn, that haunted his days and bedeviled his nights, that ruined him for anyone else.

She gave a shaky, self-conscious laugh. "I'm sorry," she repeated. It's just—" she twisted around, a tremulous, apologetic smile on her full mouth as she finally raised her eyes to him "—he's all I—oh!" Her face drained of color, leaving her skin sickly pale beneath her smooth golden tan. "Oh . . . *no*."

His mouth twisted at her reaction. "Hello, Annie."

"Gavin." She stumbled back a pace.

The child, clutched tightly in her arms, squirmed restlessly. "Mama!" he complained. "You're squishing me!"

Mama? Gavin frowned, a V forming between his brows. His gaze skated over her, snagging on her slender hands, which were clasped together to support the child's weight. An embossed silver-on-gold wedding band stood out starkly on one slim finger.

A ring he himself had slipped on her finger.

His gaze shot back to her pale face, to the stark panic she couldn't disguise.

And suddenly it all fit.

The ring, her distress, the little boy's bright blue eyes and familiar grin—

Familiar because it was the spitting image of *his*, seen captured in photos and reflected in mirrors for his entire thirty-four years.

Stunned, he stared at his wife, whom he'd last seen through the Plexiglas barrier in the penitentiary visiting room. The woman who'd sat, her expression a blank mask, and never said a word when he'd set her free to live her life without a felon for a husband. Even though, judging from the boy's size, she must have known, even then, that she was carrying *his* son.

"Down, Mama." Sam's impatient voice hung in the air. "Down, down, *down*."

Awareness flooded Gavin, first in a trickle, then in a gush, as the full extent of her betrayal crashed through him. He squeezed his eyes shut, rocked by wave after wave of fury, pain and disbelief.

A mistake, he realized too late. Because when he opened his eyes, she and the boy were gone.

One

The storm broke as Annie started for work.

Car keys in hand, she stood on her small covered porch and watched as the wind sighed through the gnarled trees that lined the dusty street. A faint drumroll of thunder echoed through the artificially early twilight, only to fade away as the first raindrops began to fall, rich with the scent of sun-baked evergreen.

She lifted her face to the breeze. It had been unseasonably hot all week. She let her eyes drift closed, the better to savor the cool wash of air that ruffled her hair and tugged at her clothes. While she no longer minded working nights, had even convinced her body it was okay to sleep from first light to mid-morning, she didn't think she'd ever get accustomed to life without air-conditioning.

A rueful smile lit her face. *Watch out, Annelise. Your silver spoon is showing.*

She sighed. Time and past, to get going. Clia would no doubt have her head if she were late.

The first thing she saw when she opened her eyes was the truck.

Big and black, its headlights gleamed in the murky light as it rolled down the street, slowing and speeding up in a way that suggested its driver was reading house numbers as he drove.

As simply as that—with an instinct she didn't question—she knew.

Gavin.

Annie had been expecting him for more than a week, ever since their disastrous encounter in the grocery store. In some ways his arrival was a relief. At least now the waiting would be over. She would see him again, and the confrontation she'd dreaded for three long years would become a thing of the past. No longer would she struggle with the guilt, the regret, the host of what-might-have-beens.

No longer would she have to look into Sam's precious little face and wonder if she'd compromised his future to survive her past.

At least now, she would *know.*

In the street, the pickup stopped altogether, then slid in against the curb with a throaty rumble. The headlights winked out; the engine fell silent. Raindrops spattered, sizzling as they struck the hood.

Oddly calm, Annie watched as the door swung open and Gavin climbed out. He hadn't changed, she thought with that strange sense of detachment. Last week in the store she'd been so overwhelmed at the sight of him she hadn't really *seen* him.

But now... Dressed in boots, jeans and a navy T-shirt, he was all man, from his hard thighs and narrow hips to his wide shoulders and strong, chiseled features. The wind snatched at his hair, tumbling the thick, inky strands across his forehead. Even from where she stood, the blue of his eyes was startling.

He started up the slight slope of her ragged lawn. His long legs made short shrift of the distance, and it was only a handful of seconds before he halted at the foot of the stairs. His gaze was shuttered as he looked up at her, taking in her work uniform of black slacks, white blouse and braided hair.

"Annie." He inclined his head a scant quarter inch.

Pain shot through her hand. She glanced down, bemused to see she had a stranglehold on her keys. Perhaps she wasn't so calm, after all. "Hello, Gavin." She forced her fingers to relax.

A faint smile twisted across the achingly beautiful curve of his mouth. "You don't look very surprised to see me." His eyes were as hard as ice chips.

Her courage almost deserted her then. "Liam Corson called me. He said you'd been making inquiries." Corson had been her father's attorney. "I—I thought you might come."

He raised one straight black brow. "And?"

"And I guess you'd better come in." She crossed the few feet to the door, opened the screen and got her key in the lock, only to falter as she heard his footsteps coming up the stairs.

Goose bumps prickled across her arms. To her horror, her hand began to shake, and the lock, always temperamental, refused to budge.

"Here." His voice sounded in her ear. She froze as he moved up behind her, unknowingly sheltering her from the wind. He reached for the key, so close she could feel the heat from his skin and taste his scent on her tongue.

And as quickly as that, she was caught in a flood of memories; of waking to the slow caress of his work-roughened fingers; of the melting pleasure she'd found in his powerful arms; of the deep, urgent murmur of his voice filling the night....

*Annie. Look at me. Look at me while I love you, baby.
See how perfect we fit together—*

The door swung open.

Annie fled inside. Pulse racing, cheeks burning, she
crossed to the battered old highboy set against the wall to
the right. She dropped her car keys and pocketbook next
to the diminutive chiming clock that had been her mother's and switched on a small ginger jar lamp. Then she
hurried across the room and turned on the larger lamp
that sat on the end table next to her yellow-and-white sofa
and the bentwood rocker—as if the light could banish the
specters of her past.

All the while she was acutely aware of Gavin, who stood
in the shadows inside the entry, silent and watchful.

Panic welled inside her. She couldn't do this, she
thought wildly. She'd been a fool to ever think she could
match his calm, his control, his icy lack of emotion—

Stop it. With a slight shudder, she clamped down on the
flow of negative thoughts and instinctively fell back on the
endless drills in deportment that had filled her teenage
years. While the Brook School for Girls hadn't taught the
proper etiquette for dealing with an estranged husband
who'd broken one's heart, Miss Kesson had repeated
countless times that good manners were always a lady's
best line of defense.

Annie was no longer certain she qualified as a lady, but
the reminder served to steady her. "Why—why don't you
come in and sit down?"

He didn't move. "You live here?"

The disbelief in his voice puzzled her, and then she understood. The little house was certainly nothing like her
father's sprawling Denver compound, or even the deluxe
town house she and Gavin had shared in the ritzy suburb
of Bretton Hills. There was just the one room, with a pair
of doors on one side that opened into her and Sam's bedrooms, a bank of windows on the other side, and an

archway at the back that led to the kitchen and bathroom.

Still, in many ways it was the first real home she'd ever known. And except for the handful of months that had comprised her marriage, the time she'd lived here since Sam was born had been the happiest period of her life.

She stood a little straighter and retreated further into formality. "Yes, I live here. Please, sit down, Gavin. I need to make a phone call, and then I'll be right with you." With that she escaped into the kitchen to call work.

Annie punched in the number she knew by heart, then braced herself.

A woman's brassy contralto answered at the other end of the line. "Yo?" she said irreverently.

Annie sagged with relief. "Nina? It's me."

There was a pregnant silence. "Shoot. Don't tell me. Your car broke down again. I'm going to personally murder that son of mine—"

"No, no. The car's fine. Really. It's just—something's come up. Can you tell Clia I may be a few minutes late?"

"Well, I can try. But I've gotta warn you, she's on a real tear tonight. Unless you're being held hostage by terrorists—which, by the way, would be considerably less scary than making her angry—you'd better get your fanny in here ASAP."

Annie's stomach sank. "Okay. I'll do my best."

"Good. I'll see you shortly. Oops—gotta run. The Wicked Witch is coming this way."

The line buzzed in Annie's ear. She replaced the receiver, trying not to think about how much she needed her job as she walked back into the living room.

There was no relief to be found there. On the contrary; it was like going from the frying pan into the fire. Gavin stood in Sam's darkened bedroom doorway, a small, slightly shabby teddy bear clutched in his hands. The look on his face stopped her in her tracks.

"The boy—your son...his name is Sam?" he said carefully.

She swallowed. "Yes."

"How old is he?"

"He was two on January the second." It was a year to the day after they'd been married; less than seven months after the Colson gates had slammed shut, destroying their marriage.

"So..." He glanced down at the stuffed animal. "He *is* mine, isn't he, Annie?"

He didn't mean the teddy bear, and she knew it. Just as she suddenly understood that, despite the stillness of his posture, the blankness of his expression, the lack of inflection in his voice, he wasn't nearly as indifferent as she'd supposed.

Yet it never occurred to her to lie. Not because she still cared about him, she was quick to reassure herself. Other than a knee-jerk response to his undeniable physical attractiveness, she didn't have any feelings left for him at all. Not after what he'd done....

No; she was doing this for Sam.

No matter what she felt, her child deserved a chance to know his father.

"Yes, Gavin." Outside, the breeze had died down; her voice seemed to hang in the sudden silence. "Sam is your son."

His head jerked up. A tremor went through him. Something flashed in his eyes, something fierce and primitive. In the next instant his control disappeared like smoke in a hurricane. "Why? Why the hell didn't you tell me?" he demanded harshly. He closed the distance between them in two explosive strides, not stopping until the toes of his boots struck the ends of her tennis shoes. "What were you trying to do—pay me back for calling it quits?"

"No!" He was so close she had to crane her neck to look up at him. "No, of course not!"

"Then what?"

She told him the only part of the truth she could. "You made it clear you didn't want a wife. I didn't think you'd want to be bothered with a child!"

"Yeah?" His face worked as he stared down at her. "Well, you thought wrong! Dammit, Annie, if I'd known you were pregnant, it would've changed everything!"

Even though it was what she'd expected he'd say, it hurt.

Yet it was a survivable pain, she realized slowly. Three years ago it would have destroyed her, but not now—not after everything else she'd been through.

She lifted her chin and gave an eloquent shrug. "I'm sorry."

"*Damn* you." Gavin wheeled away and stalked over to one of the windows, where he braced a hand against the sash and stood staring out at the deepening twilight.

She sighed, but her voice when it came was level. "I didn't do it to hurt you." To be honest, she hadn't known she *could* hurt him. "All I can say is that it's in the past. We have to go on from here."

The cotton-covered muscles in his back flexed. "Yeah? That's easy for you to say. You haven't missed out on your kid's entire life."

A half dozen retorts trembled on her tongue, chief among them a pointed reminder of where he'd been the past few years. But she swallowed it and the others, afraid to tread any deeper into the past. This was hard enough as it was. "So what is it you want?"

He turned, his blue eyes hard. "What the hell do you think?"

"I don't know," she said truthfully.

"I want to be a part of my son's life."

Annie bit back an automatic refusal, determined to remember her vow to put Sam's interests first. Still, now that the moment was at hand, it wasn't quite so easy to say the words that would allow Gavin access to her child. She took a deep breath. "All right," she said finally. "I'm sure we can work out some sort of schedule for you to visit—"

"Visit?" He shook his head. "*No*. I've already missed too damn much. I'm not missing any more."

Her breath froze in her lungs. "Then what?"

"Hell, I don't know!" He looked around, as if the answer could be found lurking in the corners. A curious expression suddenly moved across his face. "Where is he, anyway?"

"Sam?" The clock struck six, its muted chime marking off the hours. Her heart sank. She was now officially late. "He's at the sitter's."

Gavin frowned, as if only now registering the significance of having encountered her earlier out on the porch. "Why? Did you just get home from somewhere?"

She pinched the bridge of her nose, then dropped her hand. She hadn't even worked her shift, and already she was exhausted. "No, I was just going out. As a matter of fact, I'm late. Do you think we could table this until tomorrow?"

"No."

A small spark of desperation flared inside her. Though she didn't think Clia would fire her just for being late, she didn't want to find out. She couldn't afford to lose her job. "Please. It's clear we're not going to settle anything tonight."

"The answer's still no."

"But why?"

He smiled, completely without humor. "Why do you think?"

It took her a moment to correctly interpret the distrustful look in his eyes. She sighed. "*You* think. If I were going to take off, I would've done it a week ago. I swear I'll be here tomorrow. Maybe by then we'll both be calm enough to talk this through and decide what's really best for Sam."

Amazingly, the mention of their son's welfare did the trick. The suspicious gleam in his eyes flickered out, although his expression remained cool and probing. He searched her face. "What time tomorrow?" he asked finally.

The breath she hadn't known she was holding sighed out. "How about noon?" This wouldn't seem like such an ordeal after a few hours sleep, she told herself firmly. They would be able to work something out, something adult and civilized.

"The boy—Sam—will he be here?"

"Of course."

He continued to give her the same piercing stare before he nodded abruptly. "All right." He started for the door, only to rock to a stop after a few feet and look back at her over his shoulder. "But I'm warning you, Annie. Don't even *think* about running. Now that I know about my son, I'd find you."

With that he turned and slammed out the door.

Annie stood staring after him, not certain what she wanted to do more—yell, plead, throw something, or sink to her knees and cry until she didn't have any more tears.

In the end she did none of those things. She didn't have time for histrionics. Instead she grabbed her things, turned out the lights and ran for her car.

The Palomino Grill was located off Interstate 25, at the end of the freeway ramp that led to the little town of Mountainview. It was open around the clock and looked considerably better at night than during the day.

Its floor plan was simple. Booths lined three of the four walls, tables dotted the center space, and an open-ended counter with padded swivel stools stretched the length of the kitchen. An old manual cash register topped a glass-fronted counter that was filled with the usual assortment of gum, candy and antacid tablets. Garish red-and-black carpeting, sun-faded red curtains and a jukebox crowned with a decade-old display of dusty plastic geraniums completed the decor.

Annie was an hour and a half past the end of her regular shift when she dropped the tray of dirty dishes. There was a ringing crash, interspersed with the tinkle of breaking glass and the clatter of bouncing cutlery.

It might not have seemed so bad if it hadn't been the second tray she'd dropped that night.

Or if she didn't suddenly have an overwhelming urge to cry.

But it was and she did. To her horror the room began to blur, while a lump the size of one of Sam's Nerf balls bloomed in her throat.

Mortified, she stooped down, righted the tray and blindly began to pick the silverware out of the debris, stubbornly blinking back tears. She hadn't survived the past three years just to fall apart over a bunch of broken dishes, she told herself.

The reminder helped. But not nearly as much as the irreverent female voice that sounded above her head a few minutes later. "Wow. Two trays in one shift. It's gotta be BFS."

Annie glanced up at her friend, Nina. "What?"

"You know. BFS." The other waitress wiggled her fingers. "Butterfinger syndrome. Occupational hazard of waitresses, data processors and brain surgeons. Of course—" she bent down, scooped up the remaining pieces of silverware and whisked away the tray "—as far as that last group goes, the consequences tend to be an eensy-weensy bit more serious." She gave Annie a meaningful look. "Know what I mean?"

Annie stared at her thirty-something friend, looking past the rose tattoo on Nina's wrist, the improbable burgundy hair and the triple-pierced ears, to the sympathetic hazel eyes. A grateful if shaky smile spread across Annie's face. "I guess that does put it in perspective."

"You betcha." Nina set the tray aside and offered her a hand.

Annie took it. To her surprise when she looked around, she saw that the diner was empty, except for Big Bob, the night cook, and Leo, the dishwasher, whom she could see through the pass-through to the kitchen. "Where'd everybody go?"

Nina shrugged. "You should've dropped the dishes sooner. I think you scared the last group off. They lit out a few minutes ago."

"Clia's going to kill me."

Nina looked at her curiously. "Clia, my pretty, slithered onto her broom and went home hours ago. Furthermore, what she doesn't know won't hurt her."

"She'll know," Annie said firmly, "because I'll tell her."

Nina groaned. "I swear, Annie, you make Dudley Do-Right look like a piker." She disappeared through the swinging doors into the back, only to reappear seconds later, broom and dustpan in hand. She thrust the latter at Annie and began to sweep. "You really need to work on your attitude," she said without missing a beat. "Try thinking about it this way. Clia owes you for agreeing to stay until Char and May show up."

"She owes *you*," Annie said. "I was late, remember?"

Nina rolled her eyes. "Get a grip. At least you called. And it was probably only the third time you've been late in two years. Those two haven't been on time once in the

past two months. And I, for one, am getting damn tired
of covering for them."

As if on cue, the bell above the door jangled. A trio of
burly truck drivers came in, closely followed by the pair
of giggling blond twins who worked the graveyard shift.

"Finally," Nina said. She took the dustpan out of Annie's hands, gave her a quick once-over and pointed toward the far booth. "Go. Sit. We need to talk."

"But—"

"I'll be right there." Not waiting to hear any further
protest, she marched away, dumped the broken dishware
into the trash and went to have a little talk with their blond
co-workers.

She joined Annie a few minutes later. "Honest to God,
those two make Jenny's gerbil look like an intellectual."
Jenny was the second of Nina's three children; she had
one from each of her marriages. "Here." She handed
Annie a steaming cup of coffee, set her own on the table
and slid onto the seat. "You look like you could use it."

"Thanks." Annie dredged up a tired smile. "Does that
mean I look as bad as I feel?"

"Ha. You couldn't look really bad if you worked at it.
But you've jumped like a scalded cat every time anyone's
so much as hiccuped tonight. It doesn't take one of those
brain surgeons to figure out something's wrong."

"Oh."

Nina grimaced at the carefully neutral answer, twisted
sideways and stretched out her legs on the seat with a sigh
of pleasure. "So. Are you going to tell me what's going
on? Or am I going to have to pry it out of you?"

Annie rolled the cup between her hands and considered her answer.

When she'd left Denver three years ago and started
driving north, she'd been numb, so overcome by the
events of the preceding months she hadn't been able to
think past escaping the city where her entire world had

collapsed. During the previous year she'd graduated from an exclusive Boston college, returned to Colorado after a fourteen-year exile and been swept off her feet by the man of her dreams. She'd gone from being her wealthy father's golden princess, to Gavin's prized possession, to being a twenty-three-year-old orphaned ex-debutante with five thousand dollars to her name, no marketable skills, a husband who didn't want her and a baby on the way.

In the back of her mind she'd had a vague plan of starting over somewhere like Montana or Idaho. Instead the muffler had fallen off her car after a mere forty-three miles, stranding her in Mountainveiw, and she'd simply been too overcome to move on.

Yet she hadn't given up entirely. The child stirring inside had refused to let her. For the first time ever, somebody had been depending on her. Annie had been determined not to let that small, precious somebody down.

Somehow she'd found the energy and strength to rent her little house, to husband her limited financial resources through the remainder of her pregnancy, to make it alone through the long, scary hours of childbirth. Three months later she'd found her way to the Palomino, determined to do whatever she had to, to support her new little family.

Beyond the bare particulars, she hadn't talked about her past to anyone. At first because it was too painful. And then because she'd put it behind her.

Or so she'd thought.

She looked over at Nina's expectant gaze and realized she was finally going to have to say... something. She sighed, trying to decide where to start. "I ran into Gavin in the grocery store last week," she said finally.

"Gavin?" Nina's blank look spoke volumes.

"My husband. Sam's father."

"You mean, you really are... married?"

It was Annie's turn to look startled. "For heaven's sake, Nina." She glanced from her friend to the heavy gold and silver wedding band on her own hand, and back again. "*Yes*. What did you think? That I'd made it up?"

"Well...yeah. What was I supposed to think? You've been alone ever since you first walked in here desperate for a job, when Sam was just a little tadpole. You never join any of the discussions me and the other girls have about sex. I just figured some guy had given you a real bad time. That because of Sam, it was easier to say you were married than talk about it."

Bemused, Annie shook her head. "Is that why you think I've turned down every offer for a date since I've worked here?"

"Well, sure. That and the fact that you look and sound like one of those high-class types they use in ads to sell mink coats and pearls. You're light-years above the ya-hoos we get in here, and we both know it."

Annie winced, but recognized that now was not the time to dwell on what it was about her that prompted people to see the surface, rather than the person underneath. "Be that as it may, I *am* married. And Gavin is very, very real."

"So where's he been? Is he military or CIA or something?"

"No."

"Alien abduction, then?"

Annie took a deep breath. "He's been in prison."

Nina nodded. "That was gonna be my next guess." Her eyes narrowed. "So what'd he do? He didn't beat on you, did he?"

Annie shook her head, shocked at the very idea. "No. Gavin would never do that."

"So what are we talking here? Too many traffic tickets? Mass murder? What?"

Annie sighed. "The charge was accomplice to criminal fraud."

"Huh. And what does that mean in real-people English?"

"It means he worked for my father, who owned a company that specialized in building big commercial structures—high-rises, shopping malls, that sort of thing. Gavin started as a carpenter, but eventually became one of KinnairdCo's most valuable foremen. Until three and a half years ago, when a Pueblo high-rise under construction collapsed. A worker was badly injured. It turned out—" she stared into her coffee "—it turned out the company was in financial trouble. And that my father had tried to economize by substituting substandard steel and other low-grade materials for what was specified in the bid, even though he knew it could compromise the structure. Charges were brought, but before anything could be proved, he had a heart attack."

"And?"

Annie pushed her coffee mug aside and looked up. "And by then, Gavin and I had been married for three months, and Daddy had made him a partner in the business. So he—" she exhaled tiredly "—became the one held accountable."

Nina stared. "But . . . but that's not fair! How could he be blamed if he didn't know?"

"He knew," Annie said quietly. "He wasn't part of it, but at some point he found out and chose to say nothing, and that was enough to make him legally responsible as far as the Pueblo County D.A. was concerned. He came after Gavin with everything he had. On advice of counsel, Gavin pleaded 'no contest' in return for a reduced sentence. Not," she added tiredly, "that he ever discussed it with me. Verbal communication was not our strong suit."

Nina studied Annie's drawn face. "God. No wonder you left him."

Annie's mouth quirked with a faint, ironic smile. "That's just it. I didn't. *He* broke it off—" she paused "—the day I was going to tell him about Sam."

"He didn't know you were pregnant?"

Annie shook her head.

"And you didn't say anything?"

"No."

There was another long silence as Nina digested this last. "But *why?*"

Annie shrugged, no more willing to explain to Nina than she had Gavin. "It's not important."

"I see." Nina regarded her thoughtfully. "So why didn't you divorce him?"

Annie toyed with a spoon, her gaze on the dull metal handle gripped in her slender fingers. "I guess at first I hoped he'd change his mind. And then later, after I left Denver, I didn't have either the money or the energy to bother. I simply wanted to forget." She laid down the spoon and looked up at her friend. "And now . . . well, now, it doesn't matter. What matters is that he knows about Sam and he showed up at my house tonight. That's why I was late."

Nina whistled inelegantly between her teeth. "No wonder you're all shook up. So what does he want?"

"I don't know. I'm not sure he does, exactly. We're supposed to get together later today to discuss it."

Nina, hardheaded about everything else, was still a romantic at heart. "I bet he wants you back."

Annie shook her head. "No." It was the one thing she didn't doubt. "He's only interested in Sam."

Nina didn't look convinced. "How about you?"

"How about me what?"

"Do you still love him?"

"No."

Nina looked even more skeptical, but wisely didn't say so. Instead she cocked her head. "So what do you want to have happen?"

"I—I want him to go away. I want him to be a good father to Sam, but from a distance."

"Then tell him to take a hike," Nina said flatly. "And if that doesn't work, demand money. In my experience that's usually enough to make most guys take off. Look at the trio of losers I was married to."

"You don't know Gavin," Annie said, remembering his warning about leaving. "When he wants something, he's the most single-minded, determined person I've ever known."

Nina made a rude sound. "Except you."

Annie stared at her in surprise. "What do you mean by that?"

Nina reached over and patted her hand. "It means that if anybody can handle good old Gavin, it's you, hon. Open your eyes. At least where Sam is concerned, you're not some lily-livered little girl. And if nothing else—" her expression turned wry "—you've got the advantage of intelligence. After all, your hubby already proved he wasn't too bright when he let you go."

Annie's face softened. "You're a good friend, Nina," she said softly.

The redhead nodded. "You bet. Try and remember that the next time we're working different shifts and I need you to fill in for me."

"You can count on it."

They fell silent. After a few moments Nina glanced at her watch. "Lord, it's after four." She yawned and climbed to her feet. "Good thing it's Saturday. I'm going to go home and sleep a zillion hours. How about you?"

Annie stood and gathered up their coffee cups, dropping them onto the bussing cart as they went to get their purses. "First the grocery store, then sleep, then Sam." *Then Gavin.*

As if she'd heard that last, Nina reached over and gave her a quick squeeze. "It'll be okay," she said softly.

Try as she might, Annie didn't think so.

Two

He had a son.

The realization had kept Gavin up most of the night.

Yet it was only now, as he once again drove toward Annie's house, that it was really beginning to sink in.

After a week of wondering, of cautioning himself against getting his hopes up, he finally *knew*.

He had a son. A bright, bold, beautiful little boy with an angel's face and the Cantrell talent for trouble.

Joy, as fierce as anything Gavin had ever known, threatened to overwhelm him.

He took a deep breath and attempted to rein in his elation, a little uncomfortable with the strength of his feelings. Still, he couldn't help thinking it was an exceptionally beautiful morning. Last night's brief storm had passed. The sky was clear, and dawn was in full bloom, tinting the dew on people's lawns silver and painting the snow that capped the peaks to the west with lavender, pink and gold.

He had a son.

In the scheme of things, it was almost enough to balance the anger Gavin felt every time he stopped to think that if not for a quirk of fate, he never would have known of the child's existence.

Almost. But not quite.

Nor was it enough to blind him to the fact that, given last night's conversation, the boy's mother would prefer him to quietly fade right back out of the picture. Or at least limit his involvement to some nice, neat, orderly little schedule she no doubt felt she should be the one to devise.

If that was the case, she was in for a rude awakening. Although he still was a little hazy on the details, he intended to be an active part of his son's life.

With that thought firmly in mind, he slowed as he approached the small, rectangular bungalow, still a little amazed that his designer boutique wife was living in such a bargain basement place.

And then he saw the empty spot in the driveway where Annie's car should have been, and it drove every other thought from his mind. Oblivious to the squeal of protesting rubber, he hit the brake and sent the pickup skidding into the curb.

Alarm splintered through him. Yet even as his stomach twisted painfully, he told himself not to panic, not to jump to conclusions. She'd been on her way out last night. Chances were her car had broken down on the way back, or she'd lent it to a friend, or something.

She had to be here. She'd *promised,* dammit.

Heart pounding, he scrambled out of the truck. He tried the front door first, knocking hard enough to silence the birds singing in the surrounding trees. When he got no answer, he began a clockwise circuit of the grounds, stopping first to peer through the living room windows.

Inside, everything was dark and still, untouched from the way he remembered it last night.

He forced himself to step away, telling himself that it didn't mean anything as he vaulted the waist-high fence that enclosed the backyard. The first thing he saw was a small inflatable wading pool. It sat, abandoned, in the ankle-high grass, one lone rubber duck bobbing on the surface.

The sight made his heart clench.

He averted his gaze and strode across the neat concrete patio, up three shallow steps to the small service porch where he tried the back door. It was locked, as he'd expected. He leapt down, unlatched the side gate and started down the drive. It didn't take long to find that, while the shades were down on both bedroom windows, there was still enough of a gap at the bottom of each to see that neither bed had been slept in.

There was no doubt about it. Annie and the boy were gone.

Suddenly he couldn't breathe. Anger and self-disgust choked him. With a strangled curse, he planted his feet and slammed his fist into the rough clapboard siding, needing some outlet for his anguish.

He cursed the pain that radiated up his arm.

Yet it was nothing compared to the ache around his heart.

Dammit. Despite his tough-guy words, his big brave threat to track Annie down like some modern-day bounty hunter, she'd split. She'd probably taken off the minute he'd cleared the corner last night.

And to think he'd actually felt guilty about threatening her! God! He had to be the biggest fool imaginable. Hadn't he learned the hard way you couldn't trust *anyone?*

Shoulders heaving, he shook his head at the irony of it.

Until he'd seen Annie and the boy in the store last week,
he would have sworn he'd made his peace with the past.
Two years and ten months in prison gave a man plenty of
time to think. Although he would never forgive Max
Kinnaird for what the older man had done, Gavin ac-
cepted that he had only himself to blame for his own situation.

It had been his decision not to turn in his father-in-law,
his decision to allow the older man time to try and fix the
mess he'd made. The result had been disastrous, a painful reality he lived with every day.

As for his wife and his brief marriage... Well, that was
a different story. For a variety of reasons he hadn't let
himself think about Annie or the life they'd once had
from the day she'd raced out of the Colson visiting room.

He'd closed the door on that part of his past.

In much the same way, he'd also resolutely refused to
consider the future. Instead, he'd redefined his life by
simple pleasures—a cold beer, blue skies, the chance to
play a game of pickup softball after work. He'd been
thankful for the job provided by an old friend and openly
overwhelmed when the same friend had agreed to cosign
the loan to get him his pickup. He'd been fiercely grateful for every small freedom, from driving fast on the
highway, to taking his morning run, to sleeping in a room
without bars on the windows.

He'd been perfectly happy to live in the moment, a
survival strategy he'd learned in prison, where it had been
all that had preserved his sanity.

Until last week he would have said he was content.

Until last week, when the possibility he had a son had
changed everything. Suddenly he'd had a purpose again,
a reason for giving a damn.

Had apparently being the operative word, he thought
bitterly, so overcome by misery it took a minute for him
to realize that the wheezing, sputtering sound he'd been

hearing for the past thirty seconds was an approaching car.

He raised his head just in time to see Annie drive up in her ancient Honda. Shock and relief made his head swim. He straightened, anyway. By the time she'd shut off the engine, set the hand brake and climbed out of the car, he had himself under control.

Or at least that's what he thought—until he saw her undisguised wariness.

"What are you doing here?" she asked.

She was still in the same clothes she'd had on last night. He didn't want to think about the implication of that. Nor did he want to consider why her hair was mussed, her blouse partially unbuttoned, her baby-smooth skin pale with exhaustion. He took a step closer. "Where the hell have you been?"

She stiffened and lifted her chin, as if she were part of the Royal Family and he was an uncouth peasant. "None of your business." Stooping down, she reached in and grabbed a grocery bag from the passenger seat, bumped the car door shut with her hip and started along the walkway toward the porch.

Her attitude didn't do jack for his temper. "The hell it's not." He caught up with her at the stairs, which they went up shoulder to shoulder. "We had a deal, Annie—an agreement to talk."

She shoved the grocery bag into his arms, freeing her hands to work the key in the lock. "I said noon." She opened the door, snatched back the bag and looked pointedly at him. "It's not quite five-thirty, Gavin. I'm going to bed. Come back later."

The door banged shut in his face.

Stunned, he stood there a moment, then nearly ripped off the knob in his haste to get the door open. One quick glance revealed Annie wasn't in her bedroom. By the time that registered, he was already at the kitchen archway,

where he gave a quick look around, this being the part of
the house he hadn't been in last night.

Not that there was much to see. To his immediate left
were floor-to-ceiling shelves that served as the pantry and
a small Formica table with two chairs and a high chair
grouped around it. Straight ahead, beneath a bank of
windows that overlooked the tiny backyard, was the sink,
centered in a section of painted white cabinets topped by
eight feet of pale yellow countertop. The door to the
service porch was to the right.

The refrigerator was to his immediate right, followed by
another, shorter stretch of yellow counter that made a left
turn to accommodate the stove. A little further along the
same wall was the door to the bathroom.

All in all, it was like the rest of the house: spotlessly
clean but rather worn. By far the most outstanding thing
in the room was Annie, who was poised in front of the
shelves to his left.

"It must've been a real hot date," he said caustically.

Up on tiptoe to put a box of crackers away, she stiffened, shoved the box into place and sank back down. She
turned to the table, delved into the grocery sack and
pulled out a half gallon of milk. "Look. I was at work.
Okay? I stayed longer than usual because someone was
late." She crossed toward him to open the ancient fridge.

Just as a precaution—he'd had it up to the eyeballs with
her fondness for abbreviated conversations—he planted
his arms on either side of the archway. "Yeah, right." He
wasn't exactly sure why he couldn't let it go. Most likely
because it was nothing less than she deserved, after the
scare she'd given him. It sure as hell didn't have anything
to do with the fact that she looked as if she'd just climbed
out of somebody's bed. "Unless I'm mistaken, your degree is in art appreciation. What were you doing, Annie—cataloging the paintings on somebody's ceiling?"

She gave him a long look, gently shut the refrigerator, then marched over, unhooked the receiver on the wall phone, punched in a number and shoved it at him. "Ask whomever answers if I work there." She ducked under the cord and scooted past him.

"Hey, wait a minute! Where do you think you're going?"

"I told you," she said, her voice muffled as she disappeared into her bedroom. "To bed. I have four hours before I have to get Sam. We can talk then."

Her door swung shut at the same time an impatient female voice snarled into the phone. "Palomino Grill."

"Who the hell is this?" he demanded.

"The Queen of Sheba—whodya think?" This startling pronouncement was punctuated by a violent crashing sound, followed by the distinctive buzz of the dial tone.

Gavin jerked the receiver away from his ear. He'd been hung up on. Lips pursed tightly, he glared at the bedroom door and cursed. After a moment, however, he grudgingly reached out, pressed redial and waited.

This time a different voice answered. It was a man's, and it was far more congenial. "Palomino Grill."

Gavin straightened. "'Morning. I'm trying to locate Annelise Cantrell. Is she there?"

"Annie? Heck, no. You want Annie, you gotta get up early." The man chuckled at his own joke. "Call back— or better yet, come in anytime from six in the evening to two in the a.m. 'Course, you'll have to wait till Monday, 'cuz she's off for the weekend. Too bad, too—she's one fine little filly."

Gavin's voice reflected his shock. "No kidding."

"Nope. Wouldn't dare kid. The boss lady doesn't allow it."

"Well...thanks."

"Sure thing."

Gavin slowly replaced the receiver and walked into the other room. Feeling as if the world had just taken a spin in the wrong direction, he sank onto the couch, staring blindly at the closed door to Annie's room.

A waitress? Hell. She was chock-full of surprises. First the kid. Then the run-down house. Now this.

Well, what did you expect? She's her father's daughter, isn't she?

Max had been a master of the unexpected, too, he reminded himself acidly. It had been one of the crucial little personality traits of his late father-in-law's that Gavin hadn't fully appreciated until it had been too late to protect himself.

Still, even knowing what he now did about Max, Gavin had never dreamed that the old man would fail to provide for his only child. After all, she'd been the light of Max's life, the epitome of his success, his perfect, beautiful, golden girl. Nothing had been too good for her: not the fancy Eastern schools, the designer clothes, the holidays spent skiing in Gstaad or sunning on the beaches of Tahiti or St. Tropez.

God knew, the old man had wanted more for her than *him*. Gavin might have been smart enough to work his way up the ranks to become a foreman at Kinnaird Construction, might have been good enough to be considered a trusted advisor, but he'd always known that Max aspired for more than a hardworking, dirt-under-the-fingernails construction worker for his high-class daughter.

Only Annie hadn't agreed....

And this was how she'd paid for it.

He lurched to his feet. *Dammit.* The past was past. Like Annie had said last night, there was no going back. He'd done what he'd had to, what he'd believed at the time was best for both of them.

She was the one who'd chosen this path. She should have told him she was pregnant, told him about the boy. Like he'd said to her last night, if he'd known, it would've changed everything. At the very least he would've found some way to provide for her and their child.

Instead, she'd chosen to keep it a secret. To cheat him out of two and a half precious years of his son's life. A son who clearly needed him, he thought soberly, looking around. Although the children's books and toys neatly stacked on the shelves of the inexpensive entertainment center appeared to be new and of good quality, everything else in the room was well-worn, bordering on shabby.

He thought about that as he walked into the kitchen to put on a pot of coffee.

He was still thinking about it three hours and forty-nine minutes later, when the bedroom door opened and Annie padded out. Her face was flushed with sleep, her hair a tangled cloud of silver gilt that spilled over her shoulders and down her back.

She was naked except for a pale yellow cotton-knit camisole and a pair of matching bikini panties.

She skidded to a halt when she saw him. "What are you doing here?"

He returned her stare, furious at the spurt of heat that surged through his blood, the sudden stirring in his loins. "I'm waiting for that talk."

Her eyes widened as she registered the mug clutched in his hand, the proprietary way he was slouched on her sofa with his stocking feet propped on the coffee table.

He nodded toward the archway. "There's a fresh pot of coffee in the kitchen."

"How...nice," she murmured. "Why don't you make yourself at home?"

He settled more firmly into the sofa. "I intend to."

Alarm mixed with the wariness on her face. After a telling silence, she dampened her lips with the tip of her tongue. "What does that mean?"

He raised the mug and calmly took a sip of coffee before he answered. "It means," he said coolly, "that I've come to a decision about what's best for our son."

She went very still. "And what's that, Gavin?"

"Simple." His gaze never wavered from her face. "I'm moving in."

Three

———

The room seemed to tilt beneath Annie's feet. "You're not serious."

Gavin set down his mug, settled back and linked his hands across his lean, hard middle. "Oh, yes, I am."

The way he said it made her skin prickle. He sounded exactly like the old Gavin, the one who'd always gotten whatever he went after.

Yet this—this was unthinkable. "But the house is so small. There's no spare room...." She raked her hair away from her face, verbally grasping at straws while she struggled to clear her sleep-fogged mind.

His gaze followed the movement of her hand, up, then down, and the strong, masculine line of his mouth flattened out. Before she could divine his intention, he reached toward the rocker, snagged the shirt draped across the seat and tossed it at her. One black brow slashed up sardonically. "Why don't you put that on? I wouldn't want you to catch cold or anything."

Like a slap in the face, the comment brought her completely awake. She grabbed for the shirt and snatched it out of the air, painfully aware not only of the brevity of her attire, but that beneath her clinging camisole, her nipples were tightly, unmistakably beaded.

Heat burned in her cheeks. At the same time a shiver went through her, although, until this moment, she hadn't been aware she was cold. With hands that trembled, she slid her arms gratefully into the soft flannel, only to still as the sleeves tumbled over her fingertips, the shirttail drifted down her thighs, and Gavin's scent—soap, fresh air, a hint of freshly milled wood and him—wafted around her.

Too late she realized the flannel shirt was *his,* the one he'd been wearing earlier over his T-shirt.

Instantly she lifted her shoulders to shrug off the garment, only to stop as she glanced up and found him watching. His expression was as cool as ever, but there was a hint of challenge in his celestial blue eyes. It suggested he fully expected her to reject his offering like the shy, timid little virgin she'd been when he married her, a woman who'd only ever known one lover.

Him.

So, Annelise? scoffed a mocking little voice in her head. *That's precisely what you are.*

Yes. But she was damned if she'd broadcast the fact to him. Not after the way he'd tossed her aside like yesterday's newspaper. *Let him at least wonder*, insisted her shattered pride.

She forced a smile to her lips, freed a hand and rolled up one cuff, then the other, lifted her arms and flipped her hair free of the upturned collar. "Thanks. That does feel better." With what she hoped was the air of a woman who regularly entertained men while wearing nothing but their shirt and her underwear, she walked over, curled up in the rocker and tried to appear unfazed. "But you still can't move in."

His face might have been carved from stone. Except for a slight pulse visible at the base of his throat, he showed no emotion at all. "Why? Because this place is so small?" He leaned back and shrugged, dismissing her objection with an indolent gesture that made the beautifully curved muscle in his shoulders round. "So we'll find someplace bigger."

"No," she said flatly. "This is my home. I'm not giving it up. And there is no more *we*. Remember?"

She would never forget. His words were burned on her heart, scored by a thousand tears. *It's over, Annie. You were just a pretty trophy, a way to show how far up I'd come in the world. I don't want to see you back at Colson again.*

She brought up her chin. "I wouldn't live with you in a place the size of Buckingham Palace."

His jaw tightened. "Yeah? Well, pardon the hell out of me, but I didn't think your personal comfort, or mine, was the issue. I thought it was Sam's welfare we were supposed to consider. With me here, at least he'd get to stay home at night and sleep in his own bed—not get stashed God knows where. Or don't you care about that?"

Indignation blazed through her. "Don't you dare speak to me about caring! You don't have a clue what I've gone through to make a home for Sam these past few years."

His blue eyes darkened. "And whose fault is that, Annie?"

"Yours," she said flatly.

Their gazes clashed, and for a moment she was sure she'd gone too far, that he'd lash back.

Instead, after a taut silence, he was the first to look away. True, it was to glance pointedly around, his expression less than flattering as it encompassed the room and its furnishings before coming to rest on her face. But still, it was something.

"Come on. Be reasonable," he said gruffly, his tone a fraction less chilly, a trifle more persuading than it had been before. "This is hardly the lap of luxury. I've got a steady job, and I'm making good money. Think of all the things we can do for our son if we pool our resources. Not to mention how much better it'll be for him to have both of us watching out for him."

For a moment she actually wavered. Not because he was making an effort to be reasonable. And not because of the money, either, although it would be a relief to have something left over at the end of the month to set aside for emergencies.

No, it was the last part of his statement that almost made her give in. Because the truth was that his presence would alleviate the constant fear she'd lived with since Sam's birth, about who would take care of her little boy if something were to happen to her.

And then Gavin drummed his fingers against his thigh, and she noticed he was no longer wearing his wedding ring. Furthermore, given the even tan that bronzed his hand, it was obvious he hadn't worn it for some time.

Reality crashed down on her like the sky falling. What was she thinking? It was one thing to allow him to get acquainted with Sam. It was something else entirely to let him become an integral part of her little boy's life. Not when she had firsthand knowledge of the transitory nature of his devotion, the flexible attitude he brought to his commitments.

And not when she knew for herself how natural it was for a child to idolize a father, to wrongly take the blame when nothing ever proved to be enough for the man.

She didn't want that for Sam.

She shook her head. "No, Gavin. It's out of the question."

He gave her a long, unreadable look. "Is that your final word?"

"Yes."

"That's it, then." He straightened, slid his feet to the floor, reached for his boots and pulled them on. "You can't say I didn't give it a try. I guess I'll see you in court."

She was so stunned by his apparent capitulation, it took a moment for the import of that last, quietly murmured statement to penetrate. "What?"

The smile he sent her was mocking. "What did you expect, Annie? That I'd just walk away? Think again."

Her mouth felt as if she'd swallowed a handful of dust. "What—what do you mean?"

"I mean—" he climbed to his feet, towering over her as he stamped his heels down into his boots "—that I intend to be part of my kid's life, no matter what. If that means I have to sue you to establish my custody rights, so be it."

She felt the blood drain from her face. "But th-that's crazy! You'd never win."

"Why? Because I have a record?" He shook his head, a caricature of a smile still on his face. "Forget it. Besides search for you, one of the things I did this week was talk to a lawyer. According to him, the fact that I served time doesn't automatically make me an unfit parent. As a matter of fact, in his opinion, it isn't nearly as big a deal as *your* attempt to conceal my son's existence from me. Apparently, fathers' rights are a pretty hot issue these days."

Her stomach plummeted toward her ankles. "You'd do that? Drag Sam through the courts? Make him a hot issue, a bone to be fought over?" She squeezed her eyes shut, recalling the endless speculation and hounding by the Denver press that had accompanied the scandal. An ugly custody battle would be sure to revive the whole mess. She felt sick at the thought of Sam becoming the focus of such relentless scrutiny.

Gavin stared coldly at her. "Not me, Annie. *You*. All I want is a chance to be part of the boy's life. But if you want a fight—fine. I'll give you that, too. Whatever it takes."

Panic rolled through her. She felt as if she were being driven into a tight and airless corner, while he...

He looked coolly confident, as big and unyielding as one of the Rocky Mountain peaks that dominated the western horizon.

Clearly, she'd underestimated his determination.

Just as she'd overestimated her own. Not only did she not have the money for a legal battle, she simply didn't have the stomach for it. If it were only her, she might chance it. But when it came to Sam...

The possible price was too high. Even if she knew she would win, she simply couldn't risk her son's security, his happiness, his opportunity to have a normal, average home life, by making him the object of that kind of bitter fight.

And what if she *lost?* What if she were forced to share custody, to hand Sam over to Gavin for a day, a week, a month at a time? It wasn't that she thought Gavin would be an unfit parent; yet even if he qualified for Father of the Year, to Sam he would still be a stranger.

There was no escaping the truth. No matter how she felt, she had to do what was best for Sam. And what would be best for Sam would be for him to get to know Gavin here, in his own familiar home, where she could be on hand to help and watch over him.

But it would only work if it was done on her terms.

She took a deep breath. Without quite knowing how she got there, she found herself on her feet, needing to meet Gavin on a more equal level when she capitulated. "All right. You win. You can move in."

A deep, savage satisfaction lit his eyes, turning them as blue as a hot summer sky. "Good."

She smiled faintly. "On one condition."

Suspicion hardened his features in an instant. "What's that?"

"Where Sam's concerned, regarding discipline, rules, setting limits, I have the final word."

He didn't like it, but then, she hadn't expected him to. His eyes narrowed. "Why?"

She sighed. "Because he's only two and a half years old. Right now, he's testing his boundaries, and he needs consistency. I don't want him caught between us, getting two different sets of signals."

He thought about it. "Okay," he said finally, then promptly imposed a condition of his own. "That's fine...for now. As long as we can talk about it in a month or two."

In a month or... *two?* Suddenly, the enormity of what she'd agreed to slammed into her full force. She was actually going to *live* with Gavin again. They would eat off the same set of plates and drink from the same glasses. They would share a newspaper and shower in the same tub. His clothes would mingle with hers in the hamper.

She swayed, rocked by a wave of dizziness.

The next thing she knew, he'd closed the distance between them. His breath ruffled her hair. His hands grasped her shoulders.

Shock went through her. Even through the flannel, his fingers were as warm as a brand. And his touch...was achingly familiar. Her body responded instantly, a primal creature recalling its mate. Her breathing quickened, her skin warmed, her nipples tightened, her knees went weak.

For one blind, unthinking moment, she wanted nothing more than to move closer, to be held in his arms again, to recapture the sense of safety she'd once felt in his embrace.

Except that he wasn't her sanctuary anymore. He was the wolf who lurked at the door, the storm that threatened her peace—the man who'd thrown away her heart with a few, cold, calculated words.

And she couldn't afford to forget it.

"Annie?"

Her movements slow and deliberate, she shrugged off his hands, opened her eyes and forced herself to look squarely up at him. "I'm fine. Just a little...tired."

He studied her face, his own expression unreadable, before he dropped his arms and shoved his hands in his back pockets. He shrugged. "All right—if you say so. I'm going to take off, then, get my stuff together. I'll be back later."

She swallowed. From somewhere she found the strength to make her voice level, to continue to meet his hooded gaze. "Don't forget a sleeping bag. You'll need it for the sofa."

Just for an instant his eyes seemed to darken, to turn as black and dangerous as deep water. Then his expression flattened out, and he gave a curt nod. "I wouldn't have it any other way."

A moment later he was gone.

It was going to be okay.

Annie said the phrase over and over to herself all day, repeating it like a litany. It was as if some irrational, irrepressibly optimistic part of her believed if she said it often enough it might actually come true.

Now, as she stood at the front door and stared out at the gathering twilight, wondering when Gavin would finally show up, she repeated it yet again.

It was going to be okay.

That's right, Annelise. And no doubt there's some stellar person out there who'd love to sell you an ocean-front condo in Kansas, too.

She sighed. She was so tired. Of course, what with taking care of Sam during the day and working at the Palomino at night, she was *always* tired. Tonight it was simply worse than usual. She'd been so overwrought earlier, she'd been unable to rest the way she usually did when Sam went down for his afternoon nap. Consequently she was operating mainly on nerves and adrenaline, never an optimum combination.

Yet things *would* be all right. She would get through this. As Nina had pointed out, the past three years had changed her. She was no longer the naive, sheltered, emotionally needy girl she'd been four years ago when she'd returned to Colorado after so many years on the East Coast.

Nor was she the adoring stars-in-her-eyes young wife who'd been so sure that love could conquer anything.

That foolish young miss was gone forever.

Instead, she was a survivor. One who'd learned to value herself—no small accomplishment for someone who'd spent her whole life trying to please others, to live up to their image of her.

She had Sam to thank for that, she thought, her face softening as she glanced over at her son, who was crawling across the carpet, making engine noises as he recklessly drove a toy truck through a barrier of building blocks. Knowing he depended on her had given her life shape and purpose. For him, she'd found the courage and the resourcefulness to stand on her own. And those accomplishments, combined with the unconditional, unquestioning love she felt for him, had gone a long way to heal a host of old hurts.

Or so she'd thought until Gavin had insisted on moving in.

Annie took another deep breath and reminded herself
yet again that she was doing the right thing.

Besides, based on her experience with her own father,
it was more than likely Gavin would soon lose interest in
being a parent. The man she remembered had been restless and intense, not the type to sit and watch endless re-
runs of children's videos or patiently explain for the one
hundredth time why birds could fly but little boys
couldn't. Right now he was caught up in the romantic
notion of having a child, but it wouldn't take long for reality to set in. When it did, his interest would wane, and
he'd go away and leave them in peace.

In the meantime, with him working days and her nights,
they would barely see each other. Sam would have the
benefit of being home at night, of going to sleep and
waking up in his own bed. While she . . . she would finally
be able to look herself in the mirror and know she'd tried
to do the right thing.

*Look on the bright side, Annelise. Maybe you'll fi-
nally be able to get some sleep.*

Right. With Gavin here, only a room away? She'd be
lucky if she ever got a full night's sleep again.

She scrubbed at her arms, suddenly feeling chilled despite the warm temperature inside the little house. The
sound of a vehicle coming down the street drew her attention. She looked out and recognized the black pickup.
It was beginning to be as familiar as the way her pulse
picked up at her first sight of the driver.

Grateful for the camouflaging shadows, she watched
Gavin park at the curb and switch off the engine, puzzled
when he simply sat there for a moment. Although she
couldn't make out his expression, there was a suggestion
of tension about his posture, as if he, too, were bracing for
their next confrontation.

Then he climbed out of the pickup and the illusion
passed. He was freshly showered, decked out in black

jeans and a white, open-throated polo shirt that emphasized his bronzed skin and wide shoulders. He looked as arrogant, as formidable, as determined as ever as he started for the house, a small white paper bag clutched in one hand.

Annie's heart began to pound. She drew back, but it was too late. Lighter on his feet than anyone his size had a right to be, he vaulted up the steps, only to rock to a halt when he saw her.

Their gazes met through the screen.

For an instant there was nothing for her but the pure blue flame of his gaze. That, and the same whisper of memory that had come back to haunt her last night. *Annie. Look at me, baby. See how perfect—*

"Annie? Can I come in?"

She shuddered at the sound of her name on his lips. The screen door twanged, and she started to move back to put some distance between them, only to stop as she felt a familiar little body against her bare, shorts-clad leg.

She looked down to find Sam crowded close. He stared anxiously at the man silhouetted in the doorway, his bright blue eyes, the same pure sapphire color as his father's, wide and uncertain. "Mama?" He hooked a small, pudgy arm around her knee.

Damning her inconvenient memory and the heat burning in her cheeks, she reached a protective arm around him. "It's all right, bug." Despite her inner turmoil, she made sure her voice was soft and reassuring. "It's just your daddy." She felt Gavin's sharp, surprised look and wondered what he'd expected—that she'd lie, or say nothing? "Remember what we talked about earlier? How I told you he was going to come stay with us for a while?"

The child nodded, and before she could say more, Gavin hunkered down so he was more on the little boy's level. "Hey, Sam. How're you?"

Annie frowned; his voice sounded oddly husky.

Sam scooted a little closer to Annie and shrugged. "'Kay," he mumbled bashfully.

"Yeah? Well, that's good. Do you remember me from the grocery store the other day?"

Sam shook his head. "Uh-uh."

"You don't?" Gavin looked thoughtful. "How about now?"

To Annie's amazement, he crossed his eyes and stuck out his tongue.

A shy, delighted grin streaked across Sam's face. He looked down, then back up at Gavin through his long, silky lashes. "Maybe," he murmured, rocking slightly from side to side.

"Good." Avoiding Annie's gaze, Gavin settled his face back into its normal contours. "I brought you something."

Annie stiffened, her emotions leapfrogging from surprise to anger in an instant. This was something she hadn't anticipated. Expensive gifts had always been her father's answer for everything, from canceled vacations to forgotten birthdays—

"Here." Gavin opened the bag, reached in and removed a slightly lopsided ice cream cone, decorated to resemble a clown.

"Oohh," Sam cooed, "i-scream." Next to popsicles, ice cream was by far his favorite food. "I *lub* i-scream," he confided happily. Forgetting all about his shyness, he started forward with his hand out, then abruptly remembered himself. He stopped and looked up at Annie. "'Kay, Mama?" he asked hopefully, his eyes round and beseeching.

Ice cream. It wasn't some ostentatious trinket, some expensive bribe that made up in price what it lacked in thoughtfulness. On the contrary, it was a dollar-and-a-half clown cone, Machiavellian in its simplicity.

After all, what two-year-old didn't like ice cream?

Annie felt as if the floor had been yanked out from underneath her. Yet for Sam's sake, she managed to keep her voice even, to keep her seesawing emotions from showing on her face. "That's fine, sweetie. But—" she eyed the cone, which was starting to melt "—you have to eat it in your high chair, okay?"

He nodded so hard his pale gold hair lifted with the motion. "'*Kay*". He bolted for the kitchen.

Gavin straightened, still gripping the frozen treat. Their eyes met, and Annie had a sinking suspicion that if she let him see her confusion, he'd find a way to use it to his advantage if he could. "Here." Not giving herself time to think, she reached out and plucked the cone from his fingers. "Why don't you let me take that while you get started bringing in your things?" Without waiting for an answer, she turned and hurried into the other room, where Sam was busily dragging his high chair away from the wall.

She halted just around the corner. Ignoring the thin stream of ice cream that trickled across the back of her hand, she tried to still her panic, to slow her suddenly runaway pulse.

Gavin hadn't been in the door more than ten minutes, and already nothing was going the way she'd envisioned.

"Help, Mama," Sam demanded, trying to dislodge the tray so he could climb up. "Get Sam up."

"Just a minute, sweetie. Let me grab a towel and—"

"I'll get him." She gave a start as Gavin walked into the room and crossed to Sam. "What do you say, son?" He held out his arms, but made no effort to touch the child, waiting instead for Sam's permission. "You want a lift?"

There was a momentary hesitation. Sam surveyed Gavin's tall form, then glanced over at Annie, clearly looking for direction.

She gritted her teeth and nodded.

Sam gave a tentative smile that turned into a shriek of delight as Gavin reached down and effortlessly swung him high into the air before settling him into the chair.

Gavin's eyes crinkled in response. Like magic, ten years melted from his face as his lips quirked up and a pair of twin grooves bracketed his mouth. "How's that?"

A matching grin, flanked by an identical set of dimples, lit Sam's little face. "Good," he said emphatically. "I-scream now please?"

"Sure." Using his size to advantage, Gavin reached over, plucked the cone from Annie's nerveless fingers and handed it to the boy. "There you go." He turned to face her, his smile vanishing as he met her gaze. "*Now* I'll go get my stuff," he said evenly. His measured tone was at distinct odds with the challenge in his eyes.

She nodded, not certain her voice would work, pinned in place by the weight of her own turbulent feelings as she watched him disappear through the archway.

"Yum," Sam said happily, licking off half the clown's face. "Good i-scream cone."

Annie couldn't seem to breathe.

It was going to be okay.

Heaven help her. Who did she think she was kidding?

If the past few minutes were any indication, it wasn't going to be okay at all.

Four

A curious scuffling noise woke Gavin the next morning.

For a handful of seconds he didn't know where he was. Then, as he stared blankly up at the light dancing across the high ceiling, his mind began to clear.

He was at Annie's. In her living room. Where at some point in the night he must have rolled off the sofa, since he was now on the floor, his sleeping bag tented loosely over the top of him.

He gathered his wits and took stock of his surroundings.

Somebody was moving around in the kitchen. Annie, presumably, given the whoosh of running water, the rattle of pans, the gentle thump of drawers and cabinets being opened and shut.

A hollow feeling bloomed in the pit of his stomach. He shifted, telling himself it had nothing to do with her nearness, that it was merely a consequence of spending the night on the floor. After all, his only interest here was

Sam. He'd make an effort to coexist with Annie, since she was part of the package, but that was all.

As if to prove his point, he stretched, only to wince as his muscles set up a vigorous protest. No doubt about it; he was too damn old for indoor camping.

The scuffling sound that had awakened him came again. He turned his head, looked for the source—and was just in time to see his boots walk in, wearing his son.

There was no other way to describe it. Resplendent in blue pajamas, Sam had somehow managed to pull on Gavin's big buckskin cowboy boots, which were so tall they engulfed the little boy to the top of his thighs. Now he was taking a test run, shuffling precariously around the room with all the dexterity of a puppy wearing in-line roller skates.

Afraid a sudden movement might spook him, Gavin gave a noisy yawn, shifted slowly onto his side and propped his head on his hand. "Mornin', Samuel," he said softly.

It was almost too much. The boy gave a violent start and came heart-stoppingly close to clipping his head on the highboy before he regained his balance. Shaken, Gavin had to clench his fists to keep from leaping up and grabbing the kid.

Sam looked over at him, the expression on his small face a curious blend of bashful curiosity and vague apprehension. He glanced from Gavin, down at his own borrowed footgear, then back, and frowned uncertainly. "You were asleeping."

"Yeah. I was."

"Now you're not." He wagged his head back and forth.

"Nope." Gavin pushed off the sleeping bag and sat up. Clad in his navy briefs, he braced his back against the couch and stretched his legs.

Sam appeared to relax at his calm, matter-of-fact manner.

"I'm walkin'," the child informed him. He suited action to words and wobbled a few steps closer, his face scrunched into a ferocious scowl as he concentrated. "In big-boy boots," he added, in case Gavin hadn't noticed.

"Yeah. I can see that."

Sam rocked to a halt a foot away. A perplexed V formed between his pale brows as he stared at the dusting of curls across Gavin's chest. Clearly fascinated, he looked from there to the silky black arrow that bisected Gavin's belly, to the light crosshatching of hair on his arms and legs.

After a thorough perusal, he raised his gaze and made an equally complete examination of Gavin's face. "Uh-oh," he said finally. "Dada gots a dirty face."

Dada. Gavin savored the sound of it, even as he automatically ran an exploratory hand over his jaw and cheeks. He bit back a smile. "It's not dirt." He scrubbed at his chin to demonstrate. "These are whiskers."

Sam frowned. "Whiskas?"

"Uh-huh. Big boys have them. Here. Want to feel?" He reached out, carefully cupped Sam's unresisting little hand in his bigger one and pressed it to his face.

"Oh!" Sam snatched back his hand. A second later, however, he reached out and gingerly patted Gavin's chin. A grin spread slowly across his little face. "Ohhh," he breathed, looking impressed. "Ouchy."

"Sam." Annie's voice brought them both around. "What're you doing?"

Though Gavin tensed, Sam appeared completely unperturbed. "Dada gots an ouchy face," he informed her.

"Oh." Clearly taken aback by that bit of news, she glanced at Gavin, a faint spot of color appearing high on each cheek as she took in his meager attire. "I'm sorry," she said stiffly, averting her gaze. "I told him not to wake you."

"No problem," Gavin replied, abruptly falling silent as, out of nowhere, the memory of the first time he'd ever seen her slammed into him.

She'd been standing all alone in the Denver airport. Although he'd already been half in love with the pictures of her that had decorated Max's office, nothing had prepared him for the reality of her. She'd looked cool, classy, very young and very sexy in a sinfully simple, pale pink suit and high, high heels.

A faint blush had tinted her cheeks when he'd boldly walked up, explained he was there in Max's stead and introduced himself. He'd seen the flare of heat in her dark eyes that she'd been too inexperienced to hide. All of a sudden he'd realized she was as aware of him as he was of her.

The knowledge had electrified him. So had the way she'd trembled when he'd planted his hand against the delicate hollow at the base of her spine to guide her to the waiting car. That and her scent—something rich and exclusive that made him think of white lilacs and summer rain—and the silky, supple feel of her beneath his hand, had made him as randy as a stallion. He'd wanted to take her right there. He'd wanted to yank the pins out of her hair, ruck up her skirt, taste her skin with his mouth and make her *his*.

He stared hard at the woman across the room. As much as he wanted to tell himself that she looked plain, tired and nondescript in her age-whitened jeans and sleeveless denim blouse, he knew it wasn't true.

Whatever hardships she'd been through, they didn't show on her face. As for her body...well, she sure as hell didn't look like anybody's mother.

Sam obviously didn't agree. "Lookee, Mama," he piped up. "I'm wearing big-boy boots."

Annie's expression turned grave. "I see. That's nice, bug. But you know the rules. You aren't to take other people's things without asking. Especially Daddy's boots.''

Sam's face fell, taking Gavin's heart with it. Annoyed by her attempt to put a damper on the camaraderie he and the boy were enjoying, he cleared his throat. ''I told him it was okay—''

She dismissed the fib—and him—with a quick, impatient glance. ''No. You didn't.'' She turned her attention back to Sam. ''Take off the boots now, please, so you can come and eat breakfast. And next time, *ask*.''

'''Kay.'' Sam plopped onto the floor, started to tug off a boot, then paused. ''Dada come, too?'' Despite the reprimand, when he looked at Annie, his face shone with total trust.

A flicker of dismay marked her features, but she didn't hesitate. ''Of course.'' She withdrew into the kitchen.

Sam smiled, as bright and uncomplicated as the light slanting through the window blinds. He wriggled out of the boots, scrambled to his feet and set off after her, only to stop when he realized Gavin hadn't moved. ''C'mon,'' he said earnestly. ''Sam is real hungry.''

Gavin nodded at the boy. ''You go ahead,'' he said softly. ''I'll be right there.''

Sam didn't need further encouragement. He dashed into the kitchen, while Gavin climbed to his feet.

Annie might look the same on the outside, he thought as he pulled on the black jeans and white shirt he'd worn the previous day. But clearly, she'd changed. And it went a hell of a lot further than exchanging a designer suit for clothes from Value City.

The woman he'd married had been as soft, as warm and lucent as sunshine. Sam's mother, on the other hand, was cool, brusque and enigmatic, as difficult to fathom as deep water.

Oddly irritated, and not sure why, he set his boots safely out of harm's way, finger combed his hair, then padded slowly into the other room. Sam was already in his high chair, bib in place, energetically swinging his legs.

"Sam," Annie said softly, setting a helping of cut-up pancakes in front of the boy. "Behave." She nodded at the chair to the left of his high chair. "You can sit there," she told Gavin.

He nodded and made a brief detour into the bathroom. By the time he returned, feeling nominally more civilized for having combed his hair and washed his hands and face, a plateful of steaming pancakes marked his place, too. He poured himself a cup of coffee and sat, careful to keep his expression blank at the discovery that the pancakes were strangely misshapen.

"We're having Samcakes," Sam informed him around a mouthful of food. "*S* is for Sam, an' snake an' *stop!* I *lub* Samcakes."

Gavin glanced down, and the light came on as he realized the pancakes were indeed roughly *S* shaped. Surprised, he glanced at Annie, but she was too busy pushing food around her plate to notice. He transferred his gaze to Sam and felt a fierce surge of pride at the boy's obvious intelligence. "You're pretty smart, aren't you, kid?"

Sam nodded and speared another morsel of food. "Uh-huh. I'm a sweeeet-heart." He grinned at his mother, making it clear where he'd heard that particular accolade.

Annie looked up, and for a moment her face was alight with tenderness. "Yes, you are."

That hollow feeling rolled through Gavin's stomach again.

Hunger, he told himself firmly, looking away. He reached for the margarine in the center of the table and vowed to devote himself to eating. *After* he settled one small matter, however. He turned to Sam. "In the future you have my permission to wear my boots anytime, okay?" He ignored Annie's indrawn breath, waited until

Sam gave a nod of agreement, then turned his attention to his food, obstinately avoiding her gaze.

Except for Sam's occasional chatter, the rest of the meal proceeded in virtual silence until the toddler dropped his fork on the tray and pushed his plate away with a noisy clatter.

"All done," the boy announced, oblivious to the tension that stretched between the grown-ups.

Annie looked up and spoke for the first time in ten minutes. "Already?"

He nodded vigorously. "Down now, Mama? Please?" He tugged impatiently at his bib.

"All right." Annie laid down her fork and stood. "Just hold on a minute until I can get you cleaned up." Gracefully, she removed the plate, wet a clean washcloth, mopped up Sam's syrupy hands and face, took a few swipes at the tray for good measure and freed him from his bib.

"Go watch 'toons?" he asked as she lifted him down.

"All right. But just for a little while. We've got errands to run." She took a step toward the other room. "I'll turn it on and then—"

"No, no! Me! Please, please, please?"

He stared up at her earnestly. She hesitated, then nodded, and he tore out of the room. She gazed at the empty archway as if tempted to go after him. Before she could, there came a boom of sound and the unmistakable voice of Bugs Bunny thundered from the other room.

"Sam! Turn it down, please, sweetie."

"'Kay!" The volume promptly increased, rapidly approached ear-splitting level, then abruptly subsided.

She forgot herself again, and one of those breathtakingly tender smiles illuminated her face, only to vanish the moment her gaze met Gavin's. "Well," she said, the reserve back in her voice as well as her expression. She began to clear her and Sam's places. "I'd better get started on the dishes."

Gavin's eyes narrowed. It hadn't escaped his notice that she'd barely touched her food. Or that, for all the siren allure of her gentle curves, it wouldn't kill her to put on a few pounds.

Yet it was none of his concern, he reminded himself, finishing off his last pancake. The only reason he was here was to be with Sam. This inexplicable urge to look out for Annie was merely a reflex reaction, a habit left over from their brief marriage.

He scraped back his chair, picked up his plate and utensils and carried them to the sink. "You said something about errands?"

She took his things and slipped them into the warm soapy water. "Yes."

He added fresh coffee to his cup, took a sip and waited for her to say more. She didn't. He stifled a wave of irritation. "Look. If you're pouting because I contradicted you—"

She whirled. "Pouting? If Sam puts on your boots without one of us knowing and tries to negotiate the back stairs, what do you think is going to happen?" she said fiercely.

He stared at her, taken aback. She was really angry.

She rushed on. "I'll tell you. He's going to fall! And he'll be lucky if all he does is break an arm or leg. Did you stop to think about that before you gave him carte blanche to use them?"

The truth was, he hadn't, even though he'd seen firsthand Sam's struggle for balance. He could feel a hot wave of color creep up his neck. As much as it annoyed him to admit it, she was right.

Yet he couldn't quite bring himself to say so. He pursed his lips, plucked a dish towel off the counter and took a clean plate out of the drainer. "I'll talk to him," he said finally. It was the best he could do.

Her surprise was evident. "You will?"

"Yes."

She turned back to the dishes. "Oh. Well. Thank you."

He set the dried plate to one side and picked up another from the drainer. "Now. What about those errands? What do you have to do?"

"It's nothing you need to worry about."

"I'm not worried," he said evenly. "But I still want to know."

She scrubbed at the pristine nonstick surface of the frying pan. "I have to go to the Laundromat."

"You don't have a washer and dryer?"

"If I had a washer and dryer I wouldn't have to go to the Laundromat."

She had delicate hands, with long, tapered fingers. Gavin had always thought they were the kind of hands meant to play a piano or arrange flowers. Or pleasure a man....

He jerked his eyes away, angry at himself for the thought, and grabbed a handful of silverware. "Is that all you have to do?"

"No. There are a few things I need to get at the grocery store, too."

"Are you planning on taking Sam?"

She scrubbed a little harder. "Yes. He always goes with me. He likes to watch the clothes tumble in the dryers."

"How long do you think you'll be?"

"I don't know exactly. I have quite a few loads of laundry to do." She gave a casual shrug. "I guess I'll be a few hours."

"I see." He did, too. Once safely out the door, he doubted she would be back much before Sam's bedtime. Something would come up, and he would wind up spinning his wheels alone at the house while she and Sam spent the day together elsewhere. He finished drying the last of the utensils. "Tell you what." He folded the dish towel and set it on the counter. "I'm going to go take a quick shower, but I should be done by the time you're ready to go." He watched out of the corner of his eye as she tensed, and he had to suppress a grim smile. "If you want to get your stuff together," he said blandly, "I'll carry it out to the car for you."

"Oh." She exhaled, trying to hide her relief. "That would be nice. Thank you."

He shrugged. "No problem."

He didn't think she was going to be nearly so grateful when he got around to mentioning he intended to go with her.

It was something to look forward to.

Her expression carefully blank, Annie threw the last load of Sam's soiled play clothes into one of the heavy-duty washers that lined the far wall of the Rocky Peak Laundry. She was more aware than she wanted to be of Gavin leaning against the adjacent machine, arms crossed, watching her.

"So." He had to raise his voice to be heard over the mechanical clamor that filled the long, narrow room. "What do you want to do now?"

You don't want to know, she thought repressively. Despite his solicitous tone, he couldn't mask the glitter of satisfaction in his brilliant blue eyes. He knew very well he'd outwitted her with his last-minute decision to come along.

He raised one smooth black eyebrow. "Well?"

"There's a small park around the corner." Her throat was so tight she could barely get the words out. She swallowed, reminding herself yet again that she could handle this. "Sam and I usually go there to wait." It was one of her favorite places, since she'd spent an extended amount of time there when Sam had been in diapers. She wasn't wild about having to share it, but it would definitely be better than spending more time with Gavin in such close quarters. Between their session in the kitchen, the ride over in his truck and the past twenty minutes in the diminutive laundry, Annie's nerves were shot. "I guess you could come along."

Her lack of enthusiasm wasn't lost on him. His face tightened. "Great."

Annie pretended not to notice. Instead, she closed the lid on the washer, set the dial and fed quarters into the change slot.

The washer switched on just as Sam raced by in hot pursuit of a small shelty named Cosmo, who belonged to the business's owner. Grateful for an excuse to look away, she reached out and in one smooth move, plucked the boy off his feet. "Slow down, sweetie," she said, giving him a quick hug before she set him back on the ground, "before you hurt yourself."

"Yeah." To her shock, Gavin leaned forward and scooped the boy up. He dangled the giggling toddler in the air. "You want to go to the park?"

Annie braced, well acquainted with the pitfalls of phrasing anything as a question to a two-and-a-half-year-old.

"No!" As anticipated, the two-letter word was Sam's instant reply. "No, no, no. Want down!" He kicked his feet in playful protest. "Want to play with Cosmo."

"Yeah?" A smile hovered at the edges of Gavin's mouth. "How about if we see if Cosmo can come with us? That is—" the smile faltered as he glanced over at Annie "—if it's all right with your mom."

Again their eyes met. Only this time, Annie could see nothing in his face but the question. Sighing, she decided to be generous and give him points for trying—even if it was a little after the fact. "It's fine with me, but you'll have to ask Mrs. Benedetto."

"Come on, then." Gavin set Sam down, and the two of them went off to confer with the dog's owner.

Annie stayed where she was, tangled in a web of conflicting feelings.

Mostly she was surprised, she decided. She was surprised by the hands-on quality of Gavin's interest in Sam, by his apparent desire to really get to know their child. She was even more surprised that he'd made an effort to meet her halfway, to consult her, even if it was only about taking a dog to a park. Just as she'd been genuinely amazed earlier, when he'd actually acknowledged, in a half-baked sort of way, that she had a point about the boots.

The man she'd married would never have been so openminded. And not just because he'd been so self-assured he'd bordered on being arrogant, although he had been. But because he'd always been so driven, so focused on what he wanted, he probably wouldn't have stopped to really listen to her in the first place.

Not that it mattered, she reminded herself. The only thing that would ever matter between her and Gavin again was Sam.

"C'mon, Mama." Sam tugged impatiently on her shirt, putting an end to her reverie. She looked over to see Gavin waiting at the door, a leashed Cosmo dancing around him. He said a soft word, and the dog abruptly came to heel at his side, staring up at him in quivering adoration. He reached down and gently stroked the animal's head.

Annie felt an unexpected quiver of her own. Dismayed, she looked away, shifting her attention to Sam's happy face. She held out her hand and he took it, and suddenly she felt more like herself. "Let's go, bug."

The park occupied the lot between Mountainview's only movie theater and the local branch of the county library. It was small, no more than a quarter acre, and was enclosed by a wrought iron fence. Banks of summer flowers edged the paths and skirted the benches scattered strategically around the smooth green lawn. A children's play area, complete with a tree swing and a climbing toy, occupied one corner.

Once through the gate, Sam made a beeline for the latter. Released from his leash, Cosmo bounded after him, with Gavin trailing after the pair.

Annie watched for a moment. Satisfied that Sam was okay, she headed for a nearby bench, sat and lifted her face to the sun. For obvious reasons she hadn't slept well. Now she tried to put some of her worries away, to recapture a fraction of the tranquility she'd enjoyed before Gavin's reappearance in her life.

The beauty of the day helped. The sun was bright but not too hot, the air clean and clear. To the west, the Rockies were a crenelated purple wall guarding the horizon. Except for the faint sound of voices raised in song coming from the church down the street, it was quiet, a welcome change from the noise inside the Laundromat.

Slowly, breath by breath, her tension began to subside, until she finally felt unruffled enough to close her eyes.

And then Gavin sat down beside her and her fragile sense of well-being shattered.

He stretched out his legs and leaned back, his shoulder rubbing against hers. "There are some things we need to discuss."

He was too close. In addition to the solid pressure of his shoulder, his thigh was pressed against her knee, while his scent tickled her nose. She edged away, her pulse jumping. "Like what?"

He was silent a moment, his gaze on Sam, who was rolling across the grass, giggling as Cosmo tried to lick his face. "Our schedules, to start with. You work six to two?"

Relieved by the practical nature of the question, she relaxed slightly. "Yes. How did you know that?"

"The guy I talked to on the phone yesterday mentioned it."

"Oh."

He gave her a quick sideways glance. "Why those hours? Why not work days?"

To Annie, the answer seemed obvious. "So I can be home with Sam."

A flicker of surprise moved across his features, then was quickly gone. He tapped a finger against the bench top. "So. I guess that means you need to leave by what—five-thirty?"

"Yes," she said simply.

"That should work just fine, then. Most days I'm done by four or five."

She shifted sideways, the better to see him. Between the truck, his clothes and the incredible shape he was in, she'd just assumed he was doing some kind of construction work again. Yet she didn't know what, she realized. "What do you do?"

He shrugged. "I'm working for a guy I knew in high school. He's a builder, headquartered in Fort Collins. Gil does residential work, mostly new construction, some on spec, some custom. Right now we're building a house on the south side of town for a senior exec with Consolidated Mines."

"Oh." It was a far cry from ramrodding a multimillion-dollar high-rise. Yet it didn't seem to bother him, Annie realized, unsettled by yet another sign that he'd changed.

Before she had time to dwell on it, however, he'd switched the subject. "What do you want to do about money?"

"What do you mean?"

He shifted impatiently. "How do you want to split things up?"

"I don't." In truth, everything had happened so fast she hadn't actually thought about it. But then, she didn't need to. She'd come a long way during the past three years. She was proud of her job, of her little rental house, of her hard-won ability to support herself and Sam. She wasn't about to let Gavin move in and take that away.

Gavin clearly seemed to have other ideas. "What the heck does that mean?"

She forced herself to speak matter-of-factly. "I have to pay rent and utilities whether you're here or not," she said, feeling her way. That tight, intimidating look was back on his face. Anxiety knotted her stomach. "And not having to pay daycare is going to mean a huge savings for me. There really isn't any reason—"

"He's my son, too, Annie."

"Then establish a college fund or—"

"Maybe I will," he said shortly. "But that's got nothing to do with day-to-day living, and you know it."

She was silent, trying to think of a way to accommodate him that wouldn't make a substantial impact on her and Sam when he left. Finally she said uncertainly, "You could take over the insurance."

"Insurance?"

"You know. Medical, life, renter's, auto." Since she currently didn't have the first three, having him provide them would be a bounty she already knew she could live without.

He considered. "All right. As long as I buy the groceries, too. *All* of them."

"But—"

"It's only fair. I probably eat more in a day than you and Sam do in a week."

Because he was right, she acquiesced. "Okay." She watched a butterfly flutter into sight on the far side of the play area. Sam and Cosmo, who'd been busy investigating a grasshopper on the path, jumped up and pelted after it, but it remained just out of reach, floating on the breeze.

"I'll do something about your car, too—"

"No." Her protest was automatic, a reassertion of her independence. "I already have a mechanic." Jason, Nina's sixteen-year-old son, would be thrilled at the title.

"Yeah? Well, your Honda sounds as if whoever tuned it never got past the first semester of high school auto shop."

Annie bit her lip, wondering when he'd become psychic.

She glanced at him, only to have her stomach drop as he returned her gaze with an intent, probing stare that made her feel chilled despite the warmth of the day.

"What happened to all of Max's money, Annie?" he asked bluntly.

Her breath caught. It was as if a chasm had opened between them, exposing a gaping black hole that threatened to suck them in, to drag them back into the treacherous vortex that was their past.

She struggled to match his calm, to keep her voice even. "That's a pretty strange question, coming from you. You knew the business was in trouble, Gavin. Otherwise, there wouldn't have been any reason to...cut corners."

His mouth tightened. "Sure, I knew. But everything wasn't tied into the company. Max must've had some private holdings. I can't believe he didn't leave a trust fund or something for you—"

She sighed, wondering why it mattered. "He did. But by the time I paid the court fines and the lawyers, satisfied all the creditors and settled with the IRS, it was all that was left."

"So?"

"So I gave it to Calvin Russert."

He rocked back as if she'd struck him at the mention of the worker who'd been hurt in the Pueblo collapse. He stared, his brilliant blue eyes riveted to her face, unable to disguise his shock. "But why? The company had insurance—"

"Yes, but it paid the absolute minimum. There was a clause in the policy that limited liability in the event of injuries caused by fraud or actionable negligence. The sum they settled on wasn't enough to cover Calvin's rehab, so I made up the difference. It seemed little enough after what KinnairdCo cost him."

"But the money—"

"Didn't matter to me," she said firmly.

"Dammit, Annie—"

"Let it go, Gavin." She was achingly aware that he was staring at her as if he'd never seen her before.

So what else is new, Annelise?

You're just a pretty trophy, baby...

The truth was he'd turned out to be just like her father, never seeing her as a real person, with real feelings. Never thinking to ask her what *she* wanted. Never caring that the only thing she'd wanted was *him*.

She took a deep breath, reminding herself it was over, past, done. That she'd moved on.

Cosmo's agitated bark brought her back to the moment, drawing her attention to Sam. Her son's little face was red with effort as he tried fruitlessly to climb onto the tire swing, which kept scooting away from him. Already his bottom lip was beginning to quiver. Annie knew that another few minutes of frustration and he was going to start wailing—if the tire didn't smack him in the face first.

She started to climb to her feet, only to freeze as Gavin laid a restraining hand on her arm. Startled, she glanced at him.

"You mind if I go?"

She sank back, unprepared for the stark plea she could
see in his eyes. And more aware than she wanted to be of
the pressure of his warm fingers on her suddenly hyper-
sensitive flesh.

"Please?" he said quietly.

She nodded. "Go ahead."

He was off the bench in a flash, his long legs eating up
the space to the play area. "Hey, Samuel." Unlike the
guarded tone he used with her, when Gavin spoke to Sam
his voice was as soft and warm as brushed velvet. "How
about a hand?" With an effortless strength that Annie
envied, he swung the boy up and held him in the curve of
one powerful arm, murmuring something that made Sam
grin and fervently nod his head.

The boy's response seemed to lighten some of the strain
ridging Gavin's back, to lessen the taut set of his mouth.
To Annie's amazement, he reached out, grabbed the swing
chain with one hand and proceeded to hook first one long
leg, then the other, over the tire. He slid down onto the
rim and settled Sam securely on his lap. Then he walked
back as far as his long legs would take him, gave a mighty
push and lifted his booted feet off the ground.

The swing sliced through the bright summer air. Sam
gave a crow of delight. Cosmo barked again, chasing after the pair. Gavin's handsome face slowly changed, the
expression going from tense, to uncertain, to amused, to
tender.

Something inside Annie twisted.

Although she no longer loved him—and she *didn't,* she
assured herself fiercely—honesty compelled her to admit
she was...*aware* of him. Even now, after everything, when
he seemed stubbornly determined to rend the even fabric
of the life she'd created for herself and Sam, she felt a
tightness low in her belly, a tingling in her breasts, a basic
overriding awareness of her femininity—and his mascu-
linity—when she looked at him.

And, while it made her angry at herself, she was wise enough to be wary. The fact that the mere sight of him could make her pulse pick up, even now, was a clear warning.

Annie took a deep breath. There was no doubt about it. She was simply going to have to get a grip on her emotions and keep her priorities straight.

And above all else she was going to have to do everything within her power to ensure Gavin kept his distance.

Five

His mouth flat with annoyance, Gavin looked at the skeletal stairway connecting the first and second floors of the Ebersole house. He didn't need a level to tell him it wasn't quite square.

This was what he got for spending the day doing paperwork at the office in Fort Collins, he thought with disgust.

He turned to the sweaty, sunburned young man at his shoulder. "The rise and run are off. You're going to have to rip it out and recut the stair jacks."

Lee Courts looked at him as if he'd lost his mind. "What?"

"You heard me." Lee could do top-notch work when he put his mind to it, but he tended to be a little lazy.

"Aw, come on, Gavin. It's close enough to pass inspection. Nobody will ever know it's not absolutely perfect."

Gavin's jaw bunched. "You're wrong," he said in a cool, uncompromising voice. "I'll know."

Lee also had a temper. He widened his stance, his manner shifting quickly from exasperation to belligerence. "Yeah? Well then, maybe you ought to take a deep breath and try to forget. Have you thought of that? Because ever since Gil went to check out that job in Montana and left you in charge, you've been acting like somebody died and made you God."

Gavin shrugged. "Maybe. But that still doesn't mean I'm going to accept this kind of sloppy work. While Gil's gone, I'm the boss. And I say do it right."

Lee flushed. "Well, *I* say it's no big deal. *I* say it's just a little thing—"

"Little things add up."

"Yeah? Well, you'd be the one to know, wouldn't you?"

The taunt hung in the hot, still, afternoon air.

There was a sudden hush as the rest of the crew, who'd been listening avidly, not even pretending to work, sucked in a collective breath. Everybody knew Gavin was only a few months out of prison. And everybody knew why he'd been there.

Only Gavin's expression didn't change. "Nobody better," he said flatly. "That's why I'm only going to say this one more time. Either redo it or you're off the job."

The other man took in the flinty hardness of Gavin's eyes and suddenly seemed to realize how close he was to being unemployed. "Oh, all right!" he retorted, gracelessly backing down. "But only because I like working for Gil. And not before I say what everybody else is too chicken to." He stared at Gavin defiantly.

"And what's that, Lee?"

"That you've been a real jerk lately. A real surly, nitpicking pain in the butt. And we'd all be damn grateful if you could see your way clear to let up!"

Gavin refused to rise to the bait. "Okay. You've said your piece. Now go back to work." He glanced around and raised his voice. "Everybody. We've got an hour before we knock off for the weekend. Gil's not paying us to stand around."

To his relief, after a quick exchange of glances, the others nodded, murmured a few words of support and returned to their tasks. Gavin's tension subsided somewhat, and he resumed his inspection of the rest of the day's work, ignoring Lee, who couldn't seem to contain a few, last, pithy comments as he went to get a saw and a crowbar to dismantle the steps.

Gavin walked toward the front of the house and went up the main staircase, past the area where two of the men were working in what would be the master bathroom, reinforcing the corner where a whirlpool tub would go.

He took a deep breath, calming his nerves by concentrating on the work to be done. The job was right on schedule. They would finish framing today, and on Monday the roofers would come. Then they would take care of the rough plumbing, install windows and hang exterior doors, beginning the process of making the structure weathertight.

At the moment, however, the house sat in its isolated clearing like the skeleton of a great prehistoric beast, surrounded by piles of raw materials. Yet Gavin had no trouble picturing the way it would look when it was finished.

Two stories tall, it would be big and airy, with oversize windows that opened the interior to the panoramic view of the Rockies rising dramatically at its back. There would be a quartet of bedrooms, a master bath with a sunken tub, a big country kitchen, a cozy den, a family room and a children's rec room. A trio of stone fireplaces, open-beamed ceilings and lots of warm, polished wood floors would give it a distinctly Western flavor, with an emphasis on comfort.

It was a house meant for a family, Gavin thought, sawdust coating his boots. The sort of house he'd planned on owning himself someday....

He pushed the thought away and forced his mind back to the business at hand. Down below he heard the whine as Lee turned on the power saw, followed by the high-pitched scream as the blade touched wood.

Gavin shook his head. Despite Lee's bellyaching, he knew he was right to insist on having the work redone. He also knew that Gil would back him on it. The fact that his boss put a premium on quality work was one of the things Gavin liked most about working for Sheridan Homes.

Yet he also knew Lee had had a valid point. He *had* been pretty intense lately. He felt on edge, out of sorts, like a dog with a thorn in its paw that no amount of gnawing could remove.

And every day it got worse.

He tried to tell himself it was the heat. A front had moved in and stalled a few days after his and Annie's first trip to the Laundromat. The temperature had soared into the nineties every day since, taking a toll on everybody.

Yet he knew that was only a small fraction of what was eating at him.

A larger part of the problem was the job. For the better part of the past three years, his days had been laid out, his time regulated, his choices limited. Now, for this past week and part of the next, at least, he was in charge again. While he was grateful for the chance, and more moved than he wanted to admit by Gil's trust in him, the sudden responsibility was wearing him down. Hell, who was he trying to kid? He was scared. He didn't want to blow this.

Not now. Not when he had a child to support—to the limited extent the child's mother would allow him to contribute.

The thought of Annie made his mouth flatten out all over again. This would be their third weekend together, and every time he let himself consider the upcoming forty-eight hours, he tensed.

Weekdays were okay. Usually Annie was asleep when he left in the morning and on her way off to work when he got home. Like soldiers transferring the watch, or managers changing shifts, they'd spend ten or fifteen minutes conferring, exchanging pertinent information about Sam. Except for an occasional note—also about Sam—that was pretty much it.

She took care of the house, he took care of the yard. She wrote out the grocery list; he did the shopping. She fixed Sam's breakfast and lunch; he handled dinner. She paid the rent; he had them so well insured they were covered for everything from an outbreak of warts to a Martian attack.

They were a regular little pair like Ward and June Cleaver, he thought sourly.

Except they didn't talk or laugh or touch. There was no sharing of opinions, no anecdotes about work, barely any conversation at all. They didn't even fight, for God's sake, and the only time they spent together was their weekly trip to the Laundromat. And even that was in question, since last weekend Annie had offered to do his laundry for him in a transparent bid to eliminate even that limited bit of interaction. He had a feeling that if she had her way, they'd barely acknowledge each other's existence at all.

So? Isn't that what you want, too?

Gavin paused before a cutout, where a pair of French doors would eventually open onto a second-story balcony. He stared out at the snow-capped Rockies, an acid sting of panic burning through his stomach as he finally admitted he wasn't sure.

When he'd first moved in, he'd still been living in the moment. His only thought had been to be close to Sam. He hadn't considered what it would be like to live with Annie again, to smell her perfume, to hear her voice, to see her every day.

To look, but never touch.

Weekends were the hardest. They moved through the house like a pair of polite strangers. Right now, Sam was too young to notice, but that wouldn't last forever. It was clear that sometime in the not-so-distant future, something was going to have to change.

Gavin just wasn't sure what.

The realization didn't do a whole lot to improve his mood. As a matter of fact, he felt as if the thorn had just been shoved in a little deeper.

Nor was he feeling a whole lot better by the time he pulled into the driveway at the house an hour and a half later. He was late, for one thing. For another, the reason he was late was that Gil had called to say something had come up and he wouldn't be back for another two weeks.

Scowling, Gavin took one last minute to enjoy the air-conditioning, turned off the truck and braced himself for the blast of hot air to come. He shoved open the door.

The second he did, he could hear Sam howling.

"No, no, no, no."

The distraught, heartbroken sound rolled through the hushed, early-evening quiet, shrill against the soft summer hum of bees and grasshoppers.

Gavin frowned. He'd never heard Sam cry. Through some miracle of genetic blending, his and Annie's son had been blessed with an incredibly sunny nature. The kid simply wasn't given to emotional outbursts.

He clambered out of the truck and headed for the house. By the time he reached the back steps, Sam's cries had diminished from howls to sniffles, and Gavin was close enough to make out what the little boy was saying.

"No, no, no. No murk, Mama," Sam sobbed. "No murk. Juice. Want juice."

Gavin paused. All this because they were out of juice?

"Shh, sweetie. It's okay." Annie's voice was soft and reassuring. "You don't have to have milk. How about if Mama makes you some lemonade?"

Gavin's frown deepened. Things must be pretty bleak for Annie to make such an offer. While she wasn't particularly careful about her own diet, she was extremely solicitous about Sam's. As a general rule, nutrition was in, sugared drinks and junk food were out. One of her terse, businesslike notes to Gavin had been on the subject.

He opened the screen. After the bright sunshine outside, the kitchen was dim and shadowy. It took a moment for his vision to adjust. When it did, he felt as if he'd taken a punch to the solar plexus.

Annie stood in the middle of the room, Sam in her arms, an ocean of ruby red juice splashed across the floor at her feet. It was a pretty good bet she'd been getting ready for work when disaster had struck.

Because it was already a quarter past five, for one thing.

And because that would explain her state of dress. Or *un*dress, Gavin corrected, as a ribbon of heat curled through him. All she had on was an unbuttoned white blouse over a pale lace bra and matching bikini panties.

He cleared his throat and looked away. "Tough day?" He set his keys on the counter, reached down and plucked the plastic pitcher off the floor.

Annie nodded, patting Sam's back and rocking slightly in the universal rhythm of comfort. "Uh-huh," she murmured.

"What's the matter?"

"I think he's finally getting his last molar." She rubbed her cheek gently against the top of the child's silky head. "And he's got a mild case of prickly heat. And he's tired. It's so hot he didn't get much of a nap."

That explained the drawn look on her face.

Sam craned around, his little face sheened with tears. "I made a axaboo-boo, Dada," he said sadly. "The j-juice went boom." A shudder racked his sturdy little body. He sniffed, his nose stuffy from crying, and laid his cheek against his mother's shoulder.

Gavin's eyes met Annie's. She looked quickly away, but not before he saw that her eyes were also suspiciously bright.

Damn. Why did she have to be such a good mother? Not that he wanted less than the best for Sam. But she would sure be a lot easier to ignore if she would just be more shallow or less caring or something. If she would whine and complain or be cross and demanding.

"I brought home another fan," he said gruffly. "There was an extra one at the office. It should go a long way toward cooling off this place."

She continued to rock. "Thanks. That should help, shouldn't it, bug?" She pressed a kiss to Sam's pale hair.

Out of the blue, the image of the first time he'd seen her flashed through Gavin's mind again. Only, suddenly he found himself thinking that *this* woman, with her tousled hair, her tired eyes, her heat-flushed face, was a whole lot more compelling than that beautiful, biddable, unawakened princess had been.

He stiffened, appalled as he realized what he was thinking. It's the heat, he told himself fiercely. The heat, the added responsibility at work, the aftermath of his altercation with Lee. And the understandable, if displaced, lust of a healthy, red-blooded, strongly sexed man who'd lived like a monk far too long.

Yeah, right. That's why your gut cramps every time you stretch out on her bed to read to Sam and smell her scent on the pillows. That's why you come awake at first light and listen to her breathe. That's why the sound of her

*laughter makes you hard, while the tender way she looks
at your son makes you ache...*

He tore his gaze away and eyed the scarlet puddle on the
floor, trying not to notice the long length of her bare legs.
"Look. Why don't you give me Sam and finish getting
ready? I'll take care of this."

The sooner she was dressed, the better.

Annie stopped rocking. "What do you say, bug? You
want to go with Daddy?"

Sam shook his head and snuggled closer. "No. Want
Mama."

"But I have to go to work, sweetie."

Gavin heard the exhaustion in her voice. She was always tired, but for some reason, tonight it really irritated
him. It didn't take a genius to see the crazy schedule she
kept was driving her into the ground. Not that he gave a
damn for himself, but if she collapsed or something it
would be sure to upset Sam. He forced himself to focus on
what she was saying.

"I bet Daddy would let you watch 'Barney.'"

The toddler glanced over at Gavin, his expression
doubtful. "'Kay?"

God but he was a smart kid. He might only be two and
a half, but in two weeks he'd figured out his father's
opinion of a certain purple dinosaur. "Sure," Gavin told
him. He shot Annie an irritated look, thinking it was too
bad she wasn't half so perceptive. "Thanks a lot," he
murmured.

The barest suggestion of a smile flashed across her face.
"My pleasure."

His eyes narrowed. This wasn't the first time he'd seen
signs she had a sense of humor. It was doubly startling
given the madonnalike purity of her face. And that he
didn't remember it from the time they were married.

But then they hadn't done a lot of talking. They'd spent
most of their time in bed.

It was as if somebody had stomped on that thorn-tender paw. All of a sudden he felt restless and out of sorts. He glanced pointedly at the oven clock. "You're going to be late if you don't get going." He reached out and plucked Sam from her arms, carefully skirting the lake of juice. He carried the boy into the living room.

By the time he got the toddler settled in front of the television and made a pitcher of lemonade, Annie had rinsed the juice off her feet and disappeared into her bedroom to finish dressing. Gavin took advantage of her absence to skin out of his work clothes and throw on a pair of shorts, stubbornly refusing to think about what she was doing behind that closed door.

He tossed his dirty jeans and shirt into his duffel bag, frowned at the thought of tomorrow's trip to the Laundromat and went to clean up the mess in the kitchen.

He'd just finished rinsing out the mop when Annie walked in, rummaging through her purse.

She faltered when she saw him. Although her expression didn't change, he would have sworn her eyes darkened as her gaze skimmed his bare torso. It was hard to be sure, since she quickly glanced away to scan the tabletop and the counters before she crossed over and did a quick visual search of the bathroom.

"Lose something?"

"Yes." She turned, looked around again, pointedly avoided meeting his gaze. "Have you seen my keys?"

"They're on the highboy." He didn't know how, but she managed to imbue her plain black slacks and ordinary white blouse with a certain flair probably undreamed of by their designers. Still, today even she looked wilted—her cheeks were flushed and a thin sheen of perspiration dotted her straight little nose.

He looked away, squeezing the excess water out of the mop with perhaps more power than was necessary. "Why don't you take the truck?"

"No."

Her quick, automatic rejection of his offer brought him twisting around. "Why not? It's air-conditioned and—"

The guarded look was back on her face. "No. Thank you."

He turned back to the sink, unnerved by the strength of the anger suddenly swirling through him. He shrugged. "Your choice."

"Yes. It is." She went into the other room. He heard the jingle as she picked up her keys, the soft murmur of her voice as she told Sam goodbye.

She came back in, headed toward the door. He could feel her looking at him as she pushed open the screen. "It was nice of you to clean up. Thanks."

In the next instant she was gone.

He watched from the window as she went down the walk, her stride lithe and loose, the sway of her hips achingly graceful. She reached down to flip the latch on the gate, and he caught a sideways view of her face, the pure profile, the thick sweep of lashes, the lush silhouette of her lips. Once through the gate, she disappeared from sight as she skirted the back of his truck to get to her little car. He heard the engine cough asthmatically. A moment later a puff of blue exhaust filled the driveway.

The mop handle snapped in his hands.

Startled, he looked down and swore. What in the hell was the matter with him?

But he knew. It was her flat refusal to take anything from him, not even something as negligible as a drive in his truck. It was that, and the damned, blank impersonal look she'd thrown at him, coupled with that excessively polite, debutante voice.

It was really starting to get to him.

Granted, his main interest was still Sam, but that didn't mean she couldn't at least unbend enough to be...what?

Warm? Friendly? Hospitable?

Well, why not? That way they could be...

What? Buddies? Sidekicks? Pals?

Yeah, right. He gave a snort of disgust and slapped the two pieces of mop on the counter.

All right, so maybe being *pals* wasn't exactly all that came to mind when he thought of her.

Hell, he wasn't sure about anything at this point.

He just knew he was damn tired of her always looking over, around and through him, instead of at him. He'd had it up to the eyeballs with the way she kept retreating behind that damnable wall of excess civility. And he was fed up with the way she avoided him whenever she could and shrank away from the most innocent contact whenever she couldn't.

Well, what did you expect? You didn't just burn your bridges when you cut her loose that day at Colson, pal. You blew them to smithereens, then you incinerated the pieces.

"Annie." The memory of his own voice seared through him. *"You're nothing but a pretty trophy, baby..."*

His mouth tightened. Okay. So the words had been harsh.

But he'd been holding on to his control that day with the thinnest of gossamer threads. He'd known he had one shot to do the decent thing and set her free. That if he blew it, he wouldn't have the strength—or the courage—to do it again.

Besides, he'd said what he had for her own damn good, to give her a chance to get on with her life. She'd been so young, so lovely. Only a fool would've expected her to wait for him, and he'd exhausted his quota of foolishness when he'd tried to take the law into his own hands.

As it was, it had taken all his strength not to demand that just once, she at least pretend she believed in him. He'd seen the doubt in her eyes; he'd known she thought he'd been in on Max's scam from the beginning, and it had torn him up inside. He would have preferred she be honest, rather than insist the way she had that she didn't care what he'd done. That she'd stand by him, regardless. . . .

He'd needed faith, not blind devotion.

And in the end, he hadn't gotten either one.

She'd left without either a word of regret or so much as a backward glance.

"Dada?"

He started, brought back to himself as a slightly sticky little hand patted the back of his leg. He looked down to find Sam anxiously staring up at him, his manner made tentative by whatever it was he saw on Gavin's face.

Gavin's priorities snapped into place. He crouched down, consigning the past to the back of his mind where it belonged.

It was the future that mattered, he thought fiercely. And right now the future had a runny nose and bright pink cheeks.

His expression softened. "What is it, Samuel?"

"Read *Zoomy Cat?*" The boy was clutching a slightly moth-eaten teddy bear in one hand, and an oversize picture book in the other.

Gavin's mouth quirked with indulgent tenderness. In one of those bizarre fixations understood exclusively by two-year-olds, the only book Sam wanted to "read" was the story of Zoomy, a zany, slightly autocratic Siamese. Gavin had already been over it so many times he pretty much had the thing memorized. "How about dinner first?"

Sam shook his head adamantly. "No."

"Sam—"

"No. Wanna read *Zoomy Cat.*" The child's bottom lip trembled, and his little face took on a tragic cast. "Please?"

Gavin lasted all of a second against that sad look. "Okay."

The little boy's smile was brilliant. He leaned forward and gave Gavin's knees a quick, spontaneous hug. "Good."

"Good yourself," he said, swinging Sam into his arms. The feel of his son's solid little body against his went a long way to restore his equanimity.

Yet even after he walked into the other room, got himself and Sam settled on the sofa and launched into his umpteenth rendition of *The Amazing Adventures of Zoomy Cat,* Gavin couldn't completely banish his vexation at Annie's continuing aloofness.

Or quit speculating about what it would take to make her really *see* him again.

Or stop wondering why he cared.

Six

Annie stood in the dappled dawn shadows of the archway and watched Gavin shave.

Limned by the light from the window over the bathtub, he looked even bigger than usual. He was naked to the waist, a white towel slung around his neck. A pair of time-worn, fleece running shorts molded his narrow hips and sinewy thighs, while his near black hair feathered over his nape in glossy tendrils, drawing the eye to the bronzed muscles that defined his back.

Unaware of her scrutiny, he leaned forward, angled his washboard belly over the sink's porcelain edge, stuck out his chin and began to scrape whiskers from his throat. The biceps and triceps in his arm bunched and rounded with each stroke of the razor.

Annie swayed, fighting the sudden yearning she had to touch him. To run her palms over all that smooth, dense muscle; to test the satiny texture of his skin with her fingertips; to lay her cheek against him and feel the strong, steady beat of his heart against her flesh. To go up on tiptoe, part her lips, taste that hard, sensual mouth—

She squeezed her eyes shut. *Stop this. Stop torturing yourself. Turn around, go back to your bedroom and try to forget this ever happened.*

It was terrific advice, she thought, opening her eyes. And under other circumstances she would do exactly that.

Only she really needed to use the room that Gavin happened to be parked in. She sighed. Lately it seemed as if even her house had turned against her.

Before, when it had just been Sam and her, she'd loved every inch of the shabby old place. She'd considered its diminutive size easy to maintain, its simple floor plan straightforward, its handful of rooms cozy.

But over the past few weeks, the rambler had began to reveal its true character. And it wasn't pretty.

The walls were too thin. When she lay in bed after her shift, she could hear every twist of Gavin's head on his pillow, each squeak of the sofa springs as he shifted his broad shoulders or narrow hips, each soft little sigh of breath that left his lips.

Added to that, the pipes groaned and the floors creaked. Despite her constant exhaustion, she would jerk awake at dawn to the sound of the floorboards squeaking as Gavin got up. She'd follow his path as he padded in to check on Sam, then tiptoed out to dress for his morning run. She'd drift back to sleep, only to snap to awareness with his return and hear the moan of water rushing through the pipes as he made coffee, shaved and showered.

Then there were the windows. There were far too many of them. To her distress she found that when she and Gavin were both home and he was outside, it was almost impossible not to walk past a window without catching sight of him. She often felt compelled to watch as he mowed the lawn, washed his truck or worked on the sandbox he was building for Sam. Consequently she couldn't help but also see him strip off his shirt, or rake a spray of inky hair off his forehead, or lope across the yard to scoop up a giggling Sam.

Of course, that might not have been so alarming if the structure's interior hadn't also begun to shrink. If, on top of everything else, the doorways hadn't become too narrow, the rooms too small, the space so congested that when Gavin was *inside*, she was always bumping into him.

Or if the rambler's design had only allowed for one more bathroom.

She tried to decide what to do. Attempt to wait until he finished? Go next door, wake Mrs. Daschel and beg a visit to the elderly lady's powder room?

Or try to act like a responsible twenty-six-year-old mother of one, instead of a faint-hearted fool struck dumb by the sight of her estranged husband?

To her chagrin Mrs. Daschel's was sounding pretty good when the decision was abruptly made for her.

"Do you need to get in here?" Gavin asked softly. He turned, the expression in his azure eyes impossible to read as his gaze drifted over her in the shadowy light.

Annie tensed, anyway. She wondered how long he'd known she was there. And why she was suddenly aware of the utilitarian nature of her pale blue sleep shirt, of how it was a far cry from the silk teddies and satin night-gowns she'd worn when they were first married.

After all, she wasn't here to be alluring.

All she wanted to do was use the bathroom. "Yes. Please."

He nodded. His movements deliberate, he set the razor aside and rinsed his face, patting it dry with the towel he drew off his neck. He bunched the damp cotton in his fist and lobbed it toward the hamper in the corner, then walked out into the kitchen. "All yours," he said, as he set about pouring himself a cup of coffee.

She sidled past, trying not to notice how strong and straight his spine was, how perfectly it divided the strong, smooth planes of his back, how it drew the eye from his solid shoulders to the downy hollow she could see in the shadow of his waistband. She closed the door and shivered, feeling as if she'd escaped some unseen danger.

She wondered at her reaction.

Their past together may have had a number of X-rated moments, but the past few weeks had been as tame as a remake of *Bambi*.

Gavin had certainly behaved himself. Just as he'd said, his focus was on Sam.

To her surprise he was proving to be a good father, willing to give their son the two commodities Annie valued most, his time and his attention. True, it was still early yet, and she supposed there was a chance that in the future he might lose interest, when the novelty of having a child wore off.

But with every day that passed, Annie didn't think so. There was nothing flash and dazzle about Gavin's relationship with Sam. He wasn't interested in showing the boy off to his friends or boasting about his accomplishments or making him conform to some standard of behavior beyond the realm of normal childhood. He saw Sam as a person, as a unique individual to cherish, not as a prized possession or a human yardstick with which to measure his success.

And it was making Annie miserable.

Oh, she was glad for Sam. She loved her son and wanted what was best for him, and having a father who loved and cherished him was certainly that.

What she wasn't happy about was how it made *her* feel.

Even though she didn't want Gavin here, she was finding it more and more difficult to be cool and standoffish to someone who had the good taste to adore her son. In much the same way, it went against all the principles of good manners that had been drummed into her to rebuff someone for trying to be nice to *her*—whether it was bringing home portable fans or washing the floor or offering to lend her his truck. She had too much experience of her own with being rejected to be comfortable spurning someone else. Even Gavin.

The irony of it wasn't lost on her.

Sighing, she washed her hands and combed her hair, took a deep breath and opened the door.

He was waiting for her. Coffee mug in hand, he lounged against the counter. "Better?"

A telltale warmth washed her cheeks. She averted her gaze, damning the all-girls-school upbringing that had left her ill prepared to deal with life's more basic details. "Yes. Thank you." Intent on escape, she started for the archway, only to come to an abrupt stop when he moved sideways, effectively blocking her way.

"You got a minute?" He took a sip of coffee, but the intense look in his eyes belied the casualness of both the question and the gesture. "Or—" his voice took on that familiar hint of challenge "—are you going to run away as usual?"

"What is it?" She refused to be intimidated.

"It's about Sam."

There was a note in his voice that made her uneasy. "Did everything go all right last night?"

"Sure." He set his mug down on the counter. "We had dinner, took a walk, read a book. Everything went fine." He hesitated, then looked away. "Well, almost. There was this one little thing...."

Annie had instant visions of gaping wounds and broken limbs. She told herself to stop being ridiculous, but took a step toward the living room, anyway. "What happened? I looked in on him last night, but I didn't see anything—"

"Hey, hold on." Gavin moved into her path, so big he was impossible to get around. "He's fine. Really. It's just…he was jumping around, trying to get something off the counter, and somehow he knocked down a tin of cinnamon. It was open, he got some in his eyes and—"

"His eyes?" Every thought except checking on Sam flew out of her head. Not giving a fig that Gavin outweighed her by a hundred pounds, she tried to push him out of her way.

He didn't budge an inch. "Annie, calm down!" He caught her by the shoulders and held her in place. *"Please?"*

She shot him an indignant look—only to freeze as she found herself caught in the potent blaze of his celestial blue gaze. Suddenly aware of his hands, hot and hard through her thin cotton shirt, she took a swift step back, then another.

He didn't even seem to notice. "Listen to me." He spaced the words out, compelling her to pay attention. "Sam's fine. I called Poison Control, and I had them walk me through flushing out his eyes. Then, just to be on the safe side, I called Dr. Dunn. She ran me through a checklist. There was nothing wrong. No swelling, no redness, no impairment of vision—"

"You should have called me," she said flatly.

"Maybe. But—"

"Why didn't you?"

"Come on, Annie." He reached up and raked his hand through his hair. "Things aren't exactly warm and fuzzy between us. And it's not as if I couldn't handle the situation. I only brought it up because I thought you ought to know. And because Sam was a little agitated about having water poured in his face. I thought you could talk to him, maybe reassure him. I don't want him to think—" he faltered "—I don't want him to think I was trying to drown him or anything."

All of a sudden Annie was aware of several things.

She was overreacting, for one, an occupational hazard of being a single parent of an only child and a problem she'd encountered before. It was hard not to be overprotective, not to want to wrap Sam in the cocoon of her love and shield him from everything. Given the loneliness of her own childhood, her sense of abandonment, she supposed it was even understandable. But she wanted something better for Sam. She wanted balance.

She took a deep, deliberate breath and forced herself to think. When she did, she realized that while she might not know the people at Poison Control, she trusted Sam's pediatrician. Dr. Dunn would have called her at work if she'd thought there was a real problem.

And so, she thought, looking at Gavin, would he. The distress darkening his face was as genuine as anything she'd ever seen. So was the contrition. With another spark of insight, she realized that for all his matter-of-fact delivery, he was blaming himself for what had happened.

His next words confirmed it. "I don't know where the cinnamon came from, but I should've seen it. I should have been paying better attention. I should have been watching Sam, instead of the damn baseball game...."

His words faded away as something spiraled to life inside her. Something even more dangerous than lust, although that was part of it.

He was close. So close she could see a dot of white shaving cream clinging to his bronzed cheek, feel the heat from his bare chest, smell the faint, musky scent of perspiration from his morning run. So close she could make out the clustered striations of turquoise, sapphire, azure and indigo that gave his eyes their incredible color.

Yet that wasn't what was making her heart suddenly slam against her ribs. That was caused by the unexpected urge she had to reach up and smooth back the lock of sooty hair tumbling over his forehead. To do whatever she could to ease the bleak look on his face.

She stumbled back yet another step. "It was me," she blurted. "I left it out."

He broke off his self-directed harangue and stared at her as if she were speaking a foreign language. "What?"

She turned away and blindly grabbed the coffee mug off the counter. "I left out the cinnamon. Sam had applesauce when he got up from his nap yesterday. With cinnamon. I must not have put it away." She took a quick, bracing swallow of coffee. "So you see, it wasn't only your fault. It—it was just one of those things that happen. Children simply get into things."

She raised the mug again, taking her time as she sipped, and asked herself what she thought she was doing. Of all the people she'd ever known, Gavin was the most self-contained. He didn't need reassurance from her. Did he?

Of course not, she told herself briskly. Nor was that what she was trying to do, anyway. She was merely trying to connect with him for Sam's sake. So that in the future, he *would* call or consult with her if something happened to their son. After all, that was why she'd agreed to let him move in in the first place....

Gradually she grew aware of a strained quality to the silence. She looked up. Gavin was staring fixedly at the mug pressed to her lips. He had the oddest expression on his face. She lowered her hand. "Gavin? What is it?"

His eyes jerked to her face. To her consternation, a muscle ticked to life in his jaw and a faint tide of red flushed his cheeks. "I don't need you throwing out platitudes, Annie," he said suddenly. "Or patronizing me. I screwed up. I said I'm sorry. Save your sympathy for someone who deserves it. Like Sam, okay?" Careful not to brush against her, he stalked toward the bathroom. "I've got some errands to run this morning, but I'll be

back around noon to take you to the Laundromat. I'd
appreciate it if you'd be ready.''

The door banged shut.

Annie stood, stunned, feeling as if she'd missed something important, and not liking it in the least. Perplexed,
she took another swallow of coffee.

That's when she realized the mug she was clutching was
his.

That her mouth was where his had been just minutes
ago.

A shudder went through her.

With a deep-seated panic she didn't want to examine,
she jerked the cup away, took a few steps to the sink and
poured out the remainder of the liquid with a hand that
shook.

She heard the shower come on and pictured Gavin
kicking off his shorts. Standing naked under the hot,
steamy water—

She set the cup on the counter with a bang.

Remember, said a mocking little voice in her head. *All
you have to do is make sure he keeps his distance.*

Right. Except she was no longer so sure that Gavin was
the danger.

It just might be that she was.

''Gavin?''

''What?''

''Could you turn down the air conditioner?''

Gavin gripped the truck's steering wheel tighter. Although he had his eyes glued to the road, he was extremely aware of Annie on the seat beside him. She was
dressed in a yellow T-shirt that made her pale golden skin
glow. And shorts—little white shorts that hugged her hips
and cinched her waist and bared an incredible length of
smooth, lithe leg.

While it was true they were getting a temporary break in the weather today, with a refreshing breeze that was keeping temperatures in the seventies, it felt plenty hot to him. "Why?"

"Because." She scrubbed her hands up and down her bare arms. "I'm cold."

He glanced at her and instantly wished he hadn't. Not only were her arms covered in goose bumps, but her nipples were also tightly budded.

"Why don't you grab one of my shirts from the back and put it on?"

"No," she said quickly. "That's all right."

Somehow, her answer wasn't a surprise. With a mental imprecation, he reached forward and turned the fan down a few notches.

"Thanks." She twisted around to check on Sam, who was in his car seat on the truck's abbreviated back seat, surrounded by their clean laundry. For one scant but endless second, her bare knee pressed against Gavin's denim-covered thigh, while her scent tickled his nose.

"How're you doing, sweetie?" she asked the two-and-a-half-year-old.

"'Kay," the boy said with a yawn.

Gavin glanced at him in the rearview mirror. Sam had been quieter than usual today, playing without his usual verve. Yet Gavin's worry that the boy might be afraid of him after last night had proved unfounded. There was no reserve in Sam's manner toward him that he could see. Nor did the boy act as if he'd been traumatized in any way. The little guy was simply tired, worn out from the trials and tribulations of the previous day.

Annie twisted back around. She appeared to turn her attention to the passing scenery. Yet they'd gone several miles before she straightened and said abruptly, "This isn't the way home."

"No."

"Where are we going?"

"I want to drop by the job site for a minute, okay?"

"Why?"

Because I can't go back to the house just yet. Not after this morning. Not when I nearly lost it when I saw you playing kissy-face with my coffee cup.

He tried not to think about it, but it was too late.

He'd wanted to replace the mug with his mouth. He'd wanted to lick the coffee off her lips and nibble at their lush, pink fullness. He'd wanted to strafe her teeth with his tongue, then thrust inside and explore her satiny inner sweetness. He'd wanted to pull her close, cup her cotton-covered breasts in his hands and stroke her nipples with his thumbs—

Well, that's just great. You don't need the house to drive you crazy. You're doing a hell of a job all by yourself.

He shifted restlessly on the seat, canted one knee in a desperate attempt to lessen the strain on his jeans, and wondered sourly if she'd catch on if he turned the air conditioner back up and aimed all the vents at his lap.

Probably. He shifted again. "One of the guys was doing some work when I left yesterday. I want to take a look at it."

She was silent a moment. "I thought you were just one of the crew."

He shrugged. "I am. But Gil, my boss, is away, checking out some property up north. I'm filling in for him while he's gone, taking care of the paperwork, trying to make sure everything goes all right."

"Oh."

He felt her studying him and waited for her to express her disbelief. After all, he hadn't been out of prison that long. She probably thought Gil was out of his mind to trust him.

"He must be extremely grateful to have somebody with your experience working for him," she said finally.

He glanced at her. He knew it didn't mean much, but he still found her comment oddly gratifying.

"What's the matter? You look surprised. Did I say something wrong?"

"No. I guess I just expected you to point out there must be other people who've been with him longer or something."

She glanced away, looking at the stands of aspen and ponderosa pine that dotted the landscape on her side of the truck. "You were always good at your job, Gavin."

Yeah. It was being the sort of man she could believe in that he'd screwed up.

The Ebersole house sat in a clearing on a five-acre plot, reached by a gravel road that would eventually be black-topped. The truck's heavy-duty shocks helped level out the ride, but it was still plenty bumpy. That didn't seem to bother Sam; by the time Gavin pulled in, the toddler was slumped in his seat, fast asleep.

Gavin switched off the engine, tapped a finger against the steering wheel and turned to face Annie. "I'll only be a minute—unless you want to come and take a look around?" He couldn't believe he'd asked.

She shook her head. "I don't think so."

Big surprise. He unfastened his seat belt with a jerk. "Fine." He started to climb out of the truck.

"Gavin—"

To his shock she reached over and laid her hand against his shoulder. Her touch was feather light, but more than enough to hold him in place. "What?"

"It's just—I shouldn't leave Sam." For a scant second, her dark eyes held his. She quickly withdrew her hand. "Maybe another time?"

"Sure." He gave her a curt nod. Careful not to wake Sam, he closed the door, grabbed a level from the tool chest bolted to the truck bed and strode toward the house.

With every step he took he asked himself what he thought he was doing. The whole idea of coming out here was to give himself some time to get this damned case of rampaging hormones under control.

And what did he do? First he asked the cause of the problem to leave the relative safety of the pickup, where Sam served as a pseudo chaperon, and tag along. And then he got mad when she refused. Swearing under his breath, he stalked up the plywood ramp that served as the project's main entry and over to the stairway.

He felt a little better after he'd examined Lee's work. Despite their disagreement, the other man had done an excellent job. Relieved, he made a quick check of the rest of the house before he finally headed back to the truck.

Annie was propped against the back fender, her ankles crossed, her face tilted up to the sun. She looked serene, peaceful—and so lovely it made his teeth ache.

She opened her eyes at his approach. "Everything all right?"

"Perfect." The truck doors were open to allow for air circulation. He walked past her and ducked his head in the passenger side to check on Sam. The boy was not only still fast asleep; he was snoring.

Gavin straightened. "What happened? Noise get to you?"

A brief smile curved her mouth. "No. I'm defrosting. And enjoying the view." As Gavin often did himself, she glanced first at the mountains, still capped in snow, then slowly surveyed the clearing, taking in the tall trees and the meadow that rolled toward the flatland in the east, covered now in a golden sea of summer-dry grass. "This is a beautiful place for a home."

"Yeah, it is." He felt a niggling of surprise. Over the brief course of their marriage, they'd attended a number of gala parties at various posh Denver estates, but he couldn't remember her ever expressing such a sentiment about one of them.

He'd always assumed her lack of comment had been because she'd taken such luxury for granted. But now . . .

He studied her. Her beautiful face was alight as she took in their surroundings. And she looked perfectly at home as she leaned against his dusty truck in her off-the-rack clothing.

"Why didn't you go back to Boston?" The question, along with several others, had been dogging him for a while.

She shrugged. "I didn't want to."

"But you had friends there." He thought of the pictures of her that had graced Max's walls. In most, she'd been attending society events like charity auctions and gallery openings with handsome, tuxedoed young men whose three-part names—Covington Brighton III, Julian Jennison Hodge, James Wilton Cannaday—bespoke old family money. "They would have helped you, found you a suitable job, probably offered you the sort of life you were accustomed to."

She looked over at him. There was something about her expression—a trace of impatience, a touch of defiance, a hint of sadness?—that suddenly made him uncomfortable. "Is that what you thought, Gavin? That I'd just pack up, go back East and pick up my old life as if nothing had happened? As if *we'd* never happened?"

His jaw bunched. She made it sound almost unsavory, a far cry from how he'd meant it.

She shook her head. "You didn't have a very high opinion of me, did you?"

The unexpected sadness in her voice pierced him to the quick. "No. That isn't true," he said slowly. "But you were so young. So accustomed to having the best. I don't know why you chose to stay here and wait tables, when there are people who would have jumped at the chance to take care of you—"

"Why? So I could wear beautiful clothes, and always do what I'm told, and hope that eventually somebody would notice that I had thoughts, feelings, desires of my own—"

He stared, totally unprepared for the raw emotion that poured from her before she abruptly fell silent and that shuttered look slammed down over her face.

"I'm sorry." She shivered and looked away, again fixing her gaze on a distant peak. "After how you spent the past few years, those must sound like pretty paltry concerns."

He shrugged, still puzzling over what he'd just heard. Knowing on some level that with a few unbridled words she'd somehow managed to alter his perception of her forever. And that he didn't like it. He didn't like it at all. "It's over. I got through it. End of story."

She looked at him, the strangest expression on her face. "Do you really mean that? You're not . . . bitter?"

"I'll never forgive Max for what he did. But I'm not going to let it ruin the rest of my life." Oddly enough, he realized he meant it. "It's the future that counts."

The silence stretched out so long a pair of birds hidden in the treetops overhead began to sing a duet. A fat bumblebee zigzagged past, intent on a patch of clover, while the sun beat down, warm and silky.

Annie finally straightened. Moving with sudden purpose, she dusted off the back of her shorts. "I think we'd better get going." She started around him toward the passenger door.

"Annie. Wait."

She stopped as she came abreast of him. "What?" A hint of breeze caught her hair and tumbled a single ribbon of gold across her cheek. Automatically she reached up and pushed it back behind her ear.

Desire slashed through him, stronger than ever. His fingers tingled with the need to replace her hand with his own. To trace that silky cheek. To rim that fragile ear. To touch her pale, sunny hair and see if a few fine strands would cling to his callused fingertips the way they used to do.

He looked from her hand to her face.

Her eyes were shuttered. Yet despite her attempt to look cool and unaffected, she couldn't hide the pulse that jumped to life at the base of her throat as she stared up at him.

He lowered his head and kissed her.

He felt her shudder as their lips met and clung. He heard her soft intake of breath as he shaped his mouth to hers and drank in her taste, her scent, her softness.

With equal parts wonder and despair, he realized that kissing her felt even better than he remembered. That her mouth was sweeter, her instinctive response to him truer, than ever before. He clenched his hands into fists, knowing that if he touched her, there was no question of how this would end. He would lay her down on the ground and kiss her until she didn't have the breath left to protest. And then he would make love to her, burying himself deep inside her, filling her with himself again and again—

"Mama?" Sam's sleepy voice sounded from the truck.

They jerked apart like a pair of guilty teenagers.

Annie pressed a hand to her trembling lips and raised her gaze to his. "We—we'd better go."

He nodded.

Without another word, she skirted around him, climbed in the truck and shut the door.

Gavin stood a moment longer, then went to join her.

Yet he could no longer ignore the alarming suspicion that had been growing in him steadily for the past several weeks.

Like it or not, he was beginning to wonder if he'd ever really known her at all.

Seven

"Hey, angel face! Order up!"

Wiggling her fingers in acknowledgement, Annie quickly finished topping off the coffee cups of the three ranchers occupying the end booth in her section.

"Thanks, hon," one of the men said automatically, his attention riveted on something one of the others was saying about stock prices.

Annie nodded but didn't speak, not wanting to interrupt. Instead, she set off to get the order. She stopped briefly along the way to refill several more coffee cups, deliver a bill to an older couple and to drop off some more packets of half-and-half to a six-year-old who seemed to think they were the perfect appetizer, much to his mother's chagrin. In the scant amount of time it took her to work her way across the room, the bell above the door tinkled twice, announcing more customers.

She scooted around the end of the counter and slid the coffeepot back on the burner. As much as she hated the heat, she had to admit it was good for the restaurant trade. The Palomino had been doing a bang-up business all month, with people coming in as much for the air-conditioning as the food. She just wished the additional tips could do more to ease the ache in her back and the pain in her tired feet.

"Well! You going to stand around all night?" Clia bumped Annie out of the way with one ample hip so she could post an order. "This isn't a parking lot."

Startled, Annie stepped back. "Sorry," she said as the diner's owner stomped past. Although the two women were roughly the same height, they would never be mistaken for one another. Clia was twice Annie's weight and bore a striking resemblance to Danny DeVito.

Annie's gaze met Nina's across the length of the room. The redhead rolled her eyes, and Annie could almost hear her friend's silent, acerbic advice. *Run, girl, run! It's Clia the Hun!*

Annie bit back a smile, loaded her order onto a tray, hefted it up and headed for the big booth in the corner and the quartet of young men waiting for their food.

The four were regulars of sorts, college boys home for the summer from CSU in Fort Collins. Although they were probably in their early twenties, Annie thought they seemed very young.

"Hey, beautiful." Steve, a brunet with wholesome, boy-next-door looks, smiled at her. "You think I could get another soda when you get time? I'm dying of thirst."

"Of course." She slid the plate with his cheeseburger and fries in front of him. "Heat getting to you?" she asked as she began to serve the other men's food.

"Naw." His bright brown eyes warmed as they slid over her. "It's the scenery in here that's making *me* hot. You sure you won't go out with me?"

She shook her head and gave him the same answer she'd been giving him for several months. "I'm married, remember?" She softened the words with a smile.

"Ah, come on. What's one little husband among friends? Tell you what. I'll get him a date of his own. Now, what do you say?"

Annie shook her head, quietly amused by his persistence. "Sorry."

"Get a clue, Brassard," one of his friends taunted good-naturedly. "She's way too classy for you."

Steve ignored him and clapped his hands to his chest in a classic gesture of entreaty. "Did I mention that I have a heart condition? That I've only got a week to live?"

"I've got news for you, buddy," came Nina's cheerful voice as she trotted up and joined the little group, "you may have a whole lot less time than that. I believe my friend said she was married."

"Nina—" Annie started to object.

The redhead nudged her with her hip. "Don't look now, hon, but you've got company."

Catching the quiet words, Steve's gaze flew from Annie to a spot behind her, his manner undergoing a rapid-fire change from flirtatious to mildly alarmed.

Annie whirled. Gavin stood less than five feet away, Sam held securely in one arm. For a split second it was as if there wasn't another soul in the room. All Annie saw was the burning blue of his gaze. It was particularly strange, given the calm, almost impassive look on his face.

If Annie hadn't known better, she would have thought he was jealous.

"Mama!" Sam said happily, shattering the suddenly tense silence. Squirming, he stretched his arms and reached for her, as if it had been days instead of hours since he'd last seen her.

She sent a strained smile to the boy at the same instant that Steve cleared his throat behind her. "Hey, listen," he said nervously, "I didn't know you had a kid. I—I was just kidding around. I didn't mean any offense, honest—"

She took a deep breath and turned. "Of course you didn't," she said firmly. "Don't give it a second thought. I'll just go take care of this and then I'll get your soda, okay?" She plastered a bright smile on her face.

"Sure," Steve said, looking relieved.

She closed the distance between her and Gavin, scooped Sam into her arms and stepped back. "Hi, sweetie." She gave the boy a quick hug, fighting for composure as she felt Gavin's gaze fix on her. She brushed back Sam's pale hair. "What are you doing here?"

"Dada tooked me bye-bye."

"That part I guessed." Bracing herself, she looked over at Gavin. "Well?" she inquired.

Appearing utterly relaxed and nonchalant, as if that strange look that he'd sent to her had never happened, he shrugged, showing off a mouth-watering display of sun-bronzed muscle. In deference to the heat he was wearing sockless tennis shoes, a pair of gray sweat shorts and a sleeveless black T-shirt. Annie was peripherally aware of the interested stares of several female diners. "I had to take a run out to the job. I've got an inspector coming Monday and there were some things I wanted to go over. And the kid here—" he reached out and tweaked Sam's button nose, the sensual line of his mouth twitching when the boy giggled "—wanted dessert. So here we are."

Annie studied him. Monday was a weekend away. The job site was at the opposite end of town, and there was a gallon of ice cream in the freezer back at her house. Yet the guarded look in Gavin's eyes made it clear he'd said all he intended to on the subject.

"Where would you like us to sit?" he said blandly.

She looked around and quickly saw that the only empty seats were at the counter. It was no great surprise. Nina called Clia's domain "the no-buy zone." Regulars knew to give the older woman a wide berth; strangers who walked in usually asked to move after she snarled at them a few times.

With Sam on her hip, Annie led the way. After the past week, there was a certain poetic justice to letting Gavin deal with her boss, she decided.

On the surface her own relationship with him had taken a turn for the better. For the past six days they'd both been more polite, cordial and agreeable than they'd ever been before—all for Sam's sake, of course.

Yet ever since they'd kissed, there'd been an underlying tension between them that was like a storm hovering on the horizon. Distant, dangerous and disturbing, it gathered strength with their every encounter, so that even the air between them seemed to feel charged and electric, to crackle with suppressed energy. Annie knew that Gavin felt it, too. Several times in the past week she'd looked up from some task to find him watching her, a strained, shuttered look on his face. And though she told herself to ignore it, deep down she had to admit that there was a part of her that got tight and breathless with his every look.

She stopped midway along the stretch of empty stools and said a silent prayer of thanks that Clia was nowhere in sight. "Go ahead and have a seat," she told Gavin, surprised to see that somewhere along the way he'd picked up a booster seat. "I've got to get back to work, but somebody should be with you in a minute. There's a menu by the sugar dispenser. And you—" she gave Sam a kiss on the cheek "—try not to drip too much ice cream on yourself."

The boy's bright blue eyes sparkled. "I *lub* i-scream," he said with an impish grin.

"Really?" She pretended absolute amazement.

He nodded. "Really, really, really!"

"Gosh. What a surprise." To the accompaniment of his giggle, Annie rolled her eyes and settled him onto the booster seat. More aware than she wanted to be of Gavin standing too close behind her, she stepped away. "I'll see you guys later," she said, making her escape.

She made a quick round of her tables, checked on several customers, handed out a few bills, then remembered Steve's soda. She headed around the counter to get it just as Clia came through the swinging doors from the kitchen.

The older woman's mouth tightened as she saw Gavin and Sam. "Why didn't you tell me I had customers?" she demanded. Not waiting for an answer, she bustled over and planted herself in front of the Cantrell men. "Whaddya want?" It sounded more like an accusation than a question.

Gavin looked at her over the top of the menu, lowered it and offered his hand. "I'm Annie's husband, Gavin."

Clia scowled suspiciously. "Girl never says a word about her husband. Thought he was dead."

Gavin's pleasant expression didn't change. "Guess you thought wrong."

"So where you been?" She narrowed her eyes and gave him a thorough once-over. "You one of those pretty boys who likes to chase other women?"

He shook his head. "I had some trouble. Now it's over."

A flicker of genuine interest lit her homely face. She propped her hands on her hips. "You a dope dealer?"

"Nope."

"A bank robber?"

He shook his head again. "Nope. Hit man. Took out my wife's former employer." A lazy smile curved his mouth. "It was considered justified, though. She was homicidally . . . rude."

Annie caught her breath. What was he trying to do? Get her fired?

She glanced at Clia. Even at a distance of fifteen feet, she could see the tide of red creeping up her boss's neck. She braced, expecting the older woman to blast him right off the stool.

Clia gave a little shudder, her face contorted, and she made a honking noise that sounded like a Canada goose. "I suppose you're right. I guess I oughta work on my manners." She thrust out her hand and took Gavin's. "Clia Marie Zambetti. Nice to meetcha."

Clia *Marie?* Annie's jaw dropped as it dawned on her that the bright red glow suffusing her employer's skin was a blush—*not* the onset of a coronary. And that the strange twist to Clia's mouth was a smile and that honking sound a...laugh.

His glorious blue eyes impossible to read, Gavin flicked Annie a lightning glance, then turned back to the older woman and resumed his conversation. "You know, I would've sworn your name was Sheba...."

Annie couldn't believe it. Suddenly she wanted to smack something. Perplexed by the strength of her feelings, she scooped ice into a glass and hit the spigot on the soda dispenser and wondered at her irritation. So Gavin was being charming. So what? It wasn't as if she hadn't known he was capable of it. Once upon a time, not that long ago, she'd thought he was the most fascinating, irresistible man she'd ever known.

Still...did he have to be so obvious about it?

She snatched up the soft drink, snagged another bottle of ketchup since she'd noticed the one in the ranchers' booth was getting low, and headed back out on the floor just as Nina scurried up.

"Annie," the redhead whispered urgently. "What's the matter with Clia? Why's her face like that?"

Annie's exasperation increased. "Oh, for heaven's sake. She's smiling, Nina—anybody can see that."

"Oh. Right. I guess it's because your husband is such a babe, huh?"

Annie pursed her lips. "Maybe."

"No maybe about it." She stared over Annie's shoulder, her gaze openly admiring. "He's a babe all right."

"Quit drooling. It's disgusting in a mother of three."

Like the true friend she was, Nina dragged her moonstruck gaze away. Her brows knit as she registered Annie's agitation. "Sorry." Her eyes—adorned tonight with three shades of purple eye shadow that clashed dramatically with her burgundy hair—narrowed suddenly. "What's the matter? He's not using that great bod to pressure you into bed, is he?" Apprised by Annie of the bare bones of her and Gavin's situation over the past few weeks, Nina bristled loyally at the suggestion.

"No," Annie said stiffly.

Nina studied her, and all of a sudden she gave a knowing little laugh. "Oh. Well. No wonder you're a wreck."

Annie's chin came up. "I am not."

"You are, too." She leaned forward, obviously enjoying herself. "You want to know what else?"

"I imagine you're going to tell me."

"You're jealous."

"Don't be ridiculous."

"Ha." Nina leaned over and gave her a sympathetic pat on the arm, then ruined the effect by chuckling. "Girl, as soon as we get a break, we are *definitely* going to talk." She hurried away.

Annie glanced at the clock that hung over the blackboard where the day's specials were posted. It was barely past eight.

Across the room Steve waved at her.

"Angel! Order up," Big Bob called.

At almost the same time she heard Sam say, "Aunt Nee-nee!"

Annie sighed and went to deliver the soft drink.

It was going to be a long night.

Gavin couldn't sleep.

It didn't seem to matter that he was tired. That he should have been out hours ago. That he'd worked a sixty-hour week, been up since dawn and had a long, eventful evening.

As the clock struck two, his mind was working a thousand miles a minute.

Flat on his back, he lay on the couch, watched the moonlight sift across the ceiling ... and finally admitted that he never should have gone to the restaurant tonight. As long as he'd stayed away, there'd been one last stubborn part of him that could continue to pretend the Annie he'd married still existed. That the woman he was living with—the quietly complex, surprisingly competent, increasingly fascinating one—was only a facade.

But he couldn't kid himself any longer.

Not after she'd given away her trust money. Not after that revealing conversation out at the job site last weekend.

And not after he'd gone to the Palomino tonight and seen how hard she worked.

He'd spent a painful hour watching her lift heavy trays and run her legs off. He'd seen her flinch from Clia's rudeness and patiently put up with the constant demands and casual familiarity of a bunch of strangers.

It had been disturbing to watch.

Hell, who was he kidding? He'd hated it. He'd wanted to take out that college kid for coming on to her. He'd wanted to tell the Queen of Sheba where to go—and it wasn't a boat ride on the Nile. He'd restrained himself in both cases, but the experience had been unsettling. Be-

cause most of all, what he'd wanted to do was yank the
apron off Annie's slim frame and hustle her right out of
there.

He tried to tell himself that it was because the job was
all wrong for her. It was like watching a delicate show
horse struggle to pull a plow uphill through a field of
boulders. The effort was gallant, the heart and the courage were there, but it was an endeavor doomed to failure.
Because eventually, inevitably, the weight of the harness,
the hardness of the ground, the sheer size of the rocks,
would win out.

Gavin knew. He'd seen the struggle his own widowed
mother had waged to raise him and his brothers. Unlike
Annie, May Cantrell Pierce was a tough, sturdy, no-
nonsense woman from a working-class background. She
was remarried now, living comfortably in Arizona. But
Gavin hadn't forgotten his boyhood years. He'd seen his
mother's constant worry, the way she'd had to scrimp and
scrape to get by, how it had worn her down and made her
old before her time. She'd been so tired, so consumed with
the mechanics of basic survival, she'd had no time for
laughter or softness, beauty or fun.

He didn't want that for Sam.

*Hell, Cantrell. Admit it. You don't want that for An-
nie.*

With that, the idea he'd been avoiding for the past week
came crashing down on him.

All this time he'd justified his decision to end their
marriage by telling himself that what he'd done had been
for her own good. That he'd merely anticipated the inev-
itable, since she was too young, too beautiful, too sheltered, to be expected to wait for him.

Yet if that wasn't true—and knowing her now, seeing
the depth of her commitment to Sam, he had to face the
possibility it wasn't—what he'd said, no matter how good

his intentions, must have seemed cruel and heartless from her point of view.

He shifted uncomfortably, not liking the idea that he'd misjudged her. Liking even less the idea stirring in the back of his brain that perhaps he'd sent her away as much for himself as for her. That he'd been afraid—

The sound of a car coming down the street saved him from having to examine the thought more completely. He reminded himself sternly that regardless of his motivations, she sure hadn't been interested in changing his mind, but somehow the reminder wasn't very comforting.

Headlights stabbed through the front window. He knew it was Annie before the car pulled into the driveway. He heard the back door open and shut a few minutes later. Next came the rustle and clink of a purse and keys hitting the counter. There was a pause, then a sigh that told him she'd slipped off her shoes. A second later the bathroom door clicked shut, followed shortly after by the sound of the shower coming on.

Gavin sagged back against his pillow, remembering another bathroom, another shower, another time....

Their Bretton Hills apartment had boasted a big, tile shower with a skylight, a triple set of shower heads and clear glass doors. He'd walked in after work one day to discover Annie standing in the enclosure, gilded by a golden shaft of late-afternoon sunlight. Her eyes had been closed, her hair slicked back, her face raised to the cascading water. Her smooth naked flesh had gleamed, slick and warm and wet as the water gushed down, sliding over every taut hill, sleeking every lustrous valley.

His pulse suddenly pounding, he'd stripped off his clothes. The tile floor had been cold beneath his feet, a delicious contrast to the heat surging through him. He'd pulled open the glass door, stepped inside, silenced her startled cry with the hungry pressure of his lips. He'd been too hot, too hard, too primed to wait.

And miracle of miracles, she'd been ready. He'd lifted her up and she'd wound her arms around his neck, arched her back, pulled him closer. Her eyes had started to drift closed....

"Annie," he'd said hoarsely, saying the words that had been a private ritual between them. "Look at me. Look at me while I love you, baby. See how perfect we fit together."

Her lashes had fluttered up and the look she'd sent him had made his heart stumble. "I love you, Gavin," she'd whispered. "I love you...."

And then there'd been nothing but silk skin and sunlight, the roar of the water rushing around him. And Annie. Sweet, hot, tight around him. As slick and wet on the inside as she'd been on the outside—

Gavin bolted upright. Shuddering violently, he swung his feet to the floor. What the hell was he doing? He didn't need a light to know his hands were shaking. Or that his mind wasn't the only part of his body that had betrayed him.

He snapped on the lamp, anyway. Swearing steadily under his breath, he found his sweat shorts. He yanked them on, clenched his teeth against the painful heaviness in his groin and lurched to his feet—

Only to falter as he heard a whisper-light footstep.

He turned.

Annie stood in the archway, dressed in nothing more than her thin white sleep shirt. Despite the dozen feet that separated them, he caught a faint trace of white lilacs, the fragrance that haunted his dreams, before the artificial breeze from the oscillating fan pushed it away.

He willed his body to behave, but he couldn't stop the renewed rush of desire that charged through him. To his frustration, it gained strength as the stream of air from the fan molded the shirt to the damp, delicately rounded contours of her breasts and hips and faithfully outlined the faint but unmistakable curve of her woman's mound.

His lungs seemed to contract.

"What are you doing up?" Oblivious to his turmoil, she glanced at Sam's closed bedroom door. "Is something wrong?"

"Everything's fine," he said hoarsely. "I thought I heard something, that's all." Yeah. Like the seams on his shorts ripping.

"Oh." As if she'd read his mind, her gaze flicked from his face to his bare chest, then down the arrow of hair that bisected his belly. Color bloomed in her cheeks. She jerked her chin up. He saw a flash of panic in her eyes—and something more, something hot, warm and wanting—before her lashes swept down. "Oh," she said again.

Apparently she wasn't as oblivious as he'd thought.

A man with a lick of sense would have stayed where he was, would have bid her good-night, would have let her go. He knew damn well he was balanced on a paper-thin edge of control.

Yet he also suddenly knew he couldn't do it. Something was riding him hard, something that wouldn't let him back off.

Not after what he'd just seen in her eyes....

"Well." With only the slightest tremor in her voice, she raised her chin and addressed a spot somewhere beyond his left shoulder. "I'll see you in the morning, then."

She started toward her bedroom.

He closed the distance between them in a few long strides, intercepting her at the door. "Annie." His fingers closed around the delicate point of her shoulder. She was so soft, so warm, so unbearably lovely.

She turned. "Gavin, don't—"

He looked from her wide, dark eyes, to the telltale pulse pounding in her silky throat, to the high, twin mounds of her breasts beneath that thin shirt. He reached down with a hand that shook and slowly smoothed the cotton over one thrusting nipple with his thumb. "Don't what?" The velvet peak beneath his fingers tightened even further. "Don't touch you? Or—" he raised his eyes and looked directly at her "—don't stop?"

"Gavin—"

"Dammit, Annie, I want you. I want you so much it's making me crazy. And I think you want me, too. I've seen you watching me." Holding her in place with the power of his gaze, he linked their hands and tugged her into his arms.

Dimly, he heard her gasp as she came flush up against him and registered the full extent of his arousal.

And then he didn't hear anything except the roar of the blood in his ears as her hands skated up, measured the hot, hard curve of his chest and twined around his neck.

His mouth found hers, and he kissed her.

Her mouth was soft, sweet, slick, smooth. The minty taste of toothpaste stung his lips, while her scent filled his head, spring lilacs on shower-warm skin.

His heart thundered. He stroked his tongue along the seam of her mouth, nipped her lower lip, then licked away the hurt.

She whimpered. And crowded closer.

He tightened his arms around her. His tongue breached her mouth, strafed against the inside of her cheeks.

His fist bunched in the back of her shirt and drew it up. He stroked the satiny back of her thigh, higher and higher, only to falter when he discovered she was wearing panties. He slipped his fingers under the lace edge, groaning with pleasure as he squeezed the cool, firm curve of her derriere in his hand.

He urged her closer. She swayed, her breath coming in gasps as she went up on tiptoe, a soft, broken little sound coming from her throat as her nipples rubbed against the rigid muscle slabbing his rib cage.

He caught her hips in his hands and pressed her up into the rigid ache tenting the front of his shorts.

She whimpered again.

Gasping for breath, he broke the kiss and looked down at her.

His heart jammed in his throat. Her head was tipped back, her kiss-swollen lips damp and parted. A pulse beat wildly in her throat.

She looked...exquisite. Ripe to be loved.

Except that he didn't want it to be like this—fast and hard, up against a wall or down on the floor. As much as he ached to buck his hips up against her and bury himself inside her, this was too important to rush.

"Annie?" His voice was hoarse, rough, needy.

Her eyelashes fluttered up. Her eyes were dazed with passion, the color of melted chocolate. She blinked and dampened her lips with the tip of her tongue. "What?"

He swallowed. "Are you sure, baby?"

The question seemed to hang in the balance between them.

She shivered, but her eyes slowly cleared, locking on his face, searching for something. "Yes," she said finally.

A bolt of sheer, primitive possessiveness flashed through him. He swung her into his arms, shouldered aside her bedroom door and strode to the foot of the bed.

With an impatient jerk he ripped the coverlet off and tossed it aside. He knelt. The mattress sagged beneath their combined weight as he laid her down.

With shaking hands he stripped off her shirt and panties.

His shorts hit the floor.

And then he reached for her.

Eight

"Kiss me," Gavin demanded.

The bed dipped under his weight as he rolled onto his back. He linked his fingers with Annie's and tugged her up and over him, settling her across his waist.

Her breath caught at the shocking intimacy of the position. His warm, muscle-slabbed chest felt like satin-wrapped steel beneath her hands as she braced herself above him. His bare belly was hard and silky against her naked thighs. "Gavin—"

"Shh. Kiss me." He reached up, tangled his hands in her hair and tugged her face down to his, groaning a little as the pebbled points of her breasts nudged against him. "Kiss me now," he whispered, nuzzling the underside of her jaw. "Because I want you so bad I'm not going to last very long this first time. And I've waited so long to taste you, to touch you, to hear my name on your lips again...."

The startling admission set her blood on fire.

She lifted her head. Moonlight painted the chiseled angles of his face. She could see his struggle for restraint in the taut stretch of his lips, in the tension pulling the skin tight over the blade of nose, in the flexion of muscle across his chest and arms.

She dipped her head and traced the line of his jaw with the tip of her tongue, following it until she found the silky spot behind his ear. There she pressed one butterfly kiss, then another, flexing like a kitten as he smoothed his fingers down her sides and over her flanks.

In the back of her mind, she knew this wasn't going to fix anything, that they were only exchanging one set of problems for another. Yet at this moment, with the velvety weight of his desire nudging against her, it didn't matter. Need trembled through her. Her breasts ached for his touch, while the core of her womanhood throbbed.

She loved him. And she wanted him. Despite the crushing hurt he'd dealt her and the emotional chasm that continued to divide them, she wanted him. She wanted him so much she felt as if she'd shatter if she had to wait another day, another hour, another minute for his touch.

He was her first and only lover, the father of the son she loved more than life. He was her husband, the man she'd promised to cherish always. It was a vow she'd made with all her heart, even if he hadn't.

And he wanted her, too. He wanted her enough that the hand he was stroking down her spine trembled; enough that his voice shook as he whispered her name. "Annie, please, baby..."

He wanted her. The knowledge didn't erase the hurt of his previous rejection, but it definitely soothed a part of it. And she'd been so alone, so long.

She lifted her head an inch and nipped the baby soft lobe of his ear.

He groaned, the dense muscle of his sides and stomach rippling between her thighs. "What kind of kiss was that?'' he demanded. Shifting restlessly, he winnowed his fingers into her hair, stroked the delicate line of her jaw with his thumbs and brought her mouth to his.

His teeth closed over her lower lip. He bit down, gentle but unyielding, laying claim to her with that tiny sting in a basic, primal way that was unbearably exciting. By the time he released her to slick kiss after kiss over the tiny hurt, she was shivering. It was a shiver that intensified as he opened his mouth over hers and stabbed his tongue inside her. Cradling her face in his strong callused hands, he initiated a rhythm that evoked the act to come.

Each kiss was harder, hotter, deeper. Annie whimpered, meeting him touch for touch, welcoming each slick thrust as a stream of wet heat began to flow through her. It arrowed down, pooling in the damp, aching, swollen spot between her thighs.

Gasping for breath, Gavin tore his mouth away. "Oh, baby. You taste so good. Hot. Sweet. I can't get enough...." He angled his head and began to blaze a trail from the point of her chin downward. He paused to lave the pulse at the base of her throat, then urged her to rise up so that he could cup her breasts in his hands. He pressed the taut globes together and buried his face against the valley he'd created. "So pretty... so soft. You smell like heaven...."

He brought up his knees, shifting her further forward. His tongue lashed out and bathed one tightly beaded nipple, then the other, back and forth until Annie didn't think she could stand another second. And then his teeth closed gently around one supersensitive tip, and the hot, wet circle of his lips latched on to her. Her back bowed and her hands bit into his shoulders. She cried out at the delicious tug of his mouth as he began to suckle.

Suddenly, she couldn't wait another moment. Her hips began to rock. Whimpering, she tried to scoot back, needing him inside her. "Now. Gavin. Please."

He didn't need any further urging. He released her nipple, flattened the angle of his legs, reached down and positioned himself as Annie rose above him. Catching her hips in his hands, he held her steady and centered her against the broad tip of his thick shaft.

Gently, she rocked her pelvis and brushed against him, the motion so slight it was almost indiscernible.

His control vanished. His hands clamped down, he braced his feet against the mattress and thrust.

Annie was slick and wet and ready. Even so, the sense of invasion was shocking. She clutched at his shoulders and bucked against him. The small of her back hollowed and a soft little cry escaped her at the power of his penetration. The cry became a gasp as he wrapped his hands around her waist and pressed her down, down, down, until he was socketed in her to the hilt.

For an instant, neither moved.

Outside, the night was warm and hushed and still. Inside, the air was hot and steamy, filled with the musky scent of their damp, trembling bodies and the harsh, raspy sound of their labored breathing.

Yet, for one endless second, their past seemed to whisper through the moonlit room.

Annie...look at me, baby...see how perfect we fit....

And then Gavin lifted her up, until he was barely still inside her, then brought her sliding endlessly, gloriously down, and they both cried out. "Ride me," he gritted out. He let go of her waist, reached up, wrapped a handful of her pale, glossy hair around his fist and tugged her down for a hard, savage kiss. "Ride me," he said again. "Please, Annelise."

"Yes..." She leaned forward, making his breath hiss as she shifted the angle of his invasion. She began to move, measuring his length inside her. She went slow at first, savoring each sensation, from the velvet slide of her tender nipples against his hard chest, to the tickle of his hair-roughened thighs against her bare bottom, to the corded velvet of his hands clamped to the back of her thighs.

Yet she couldn't keep the pace down for long. Gavin wouldn't let her. Twisting feverishly, he plucked at the sheets, his big body rigid beneath hers. "You feel so good," he told her, his voice ragged. "So wet. So tight. So right." He shuddered, his chest heaving, the ebony hair tumbling over his forehead damp from exertion. He began to drive into her, urging her to go faster, putting more and more power into each stroke of his body. "Oh, baby... I can't... I—can't—wait—"

Suddenly, he caught her by the shoulders and pushed her upright, reached down and stroked his thumb over the slick swollen center of her desire. Annie cried out as he rotated the blunt pad over the spot that ached most for his touch—once, twice, thrice. "Yes, yes, yes," she sobbed, her voice rising explosively, only to end on a wail as he unexpectedly stilled.

"Gavin. *Gavin!*"

He rotated his thumb one more time, pressed and abruptly slammed his hips upward.

Her world contracted. Like smoke sucked into a vacuum, it narrowed to the pulse point between her thighs, concentrated into a pleasure so intense it was almost painful, then exploded outward. Shaking uncontrollably, she clung to Gavin as wave after wave of sensation beat through her, flooding through her belly and breasts. The velvet glove of her body quivered and clenched, again and again, until suddenly Gavin cried out, too, a low, guttural sound wrenched from the very heart of him.

His hands jerked to her hips. Holding her against him, he arched up off the bed, his entire body shaking as he poured himself into her. It seemed an eternity before he fell bonelessly back against the mattress.

Annie promptly collapsed across his chest. Limp, sated, they clung together, too exhausted, too overwhelmed, too drained to move. It was a long while before their skin cooled, before their heartbeats began to approach normal.

Beyond the window, the darkness was beginning to lift, shading from ebony to charcoal with the dawn's approach. Some time in the past hour, a breeze had kicked up. Now it washed into the room, bringing with it a welcome breath of cool air and the scent of distant rain.

"Gavin—" Annie raised her head, her eyes meeting his in the shadowy light.

"Shh." He pressed a finger to her lips. Emotions crowded him. There were a dozen different things he wanted to say, but he just couldn't. Not now. Not yet.

It was too soon and he felt too raw. Gently, he dragged a knuckle across her silky cheek, smoothed her pale hair behind her ear, stroked his hands down the satiny soft line of her spine, trying to tell her with his touch what he couldn't put into words.

He summoned the last of his strength, reached over, hauled the coverlet up off the floor and covered them.

This wasn't the time for talk. Tomorrow—no, today, he realized—would be soon enough.

Moments later, still linked together, they were both fast asleep.

It was late afternoon when Annie awoke.

She surfaced sluggishly, emerging from sleep as if she were a diver coming up from the deepest part of the sea.

At first there was only a hazy sense of contentment. But soon she knew she was curled on her side. She could hear the theme from "Sesame Street" coming from the TV in the other room and the muffled drip of rain running off the eaves. She could smell the rain, too, as a fragrant current of air swept in the window and tickled her face.

Like a dash of water, it washed the cobwebs from her mind, bringing a rush toward awareness.

She opened her eyes, blinked in the dim light, then realized the window shade was down. Automatically she glanced at the clock on the bedside table and saw with a sense of mild shock that it was a quarter to five.

Suddenly, she remembered . . . everything.

She and Gavin had made love. More than once.

There'd been that first time, with her on top. And then a second time, shortly after sunrise, when he'd moved over her and taken her fast and hard to another explosive climax. Things got hazy after that, but she had a vague memory of him rolling out of bed, telling her to go back to sleep, that he'd take care of Sam.

She had a much more vivid recollection of his return, during what she now realized must have been Sam's afternoon nap. She remembered waking to the feel of him solid and hot along the length of her back, his hands cupping her breasts.

That time had been torturously slow, with him driving her up and bringing her to the peak of pleasure again and again and again—and her doing the same to him—before they'd finally toppled over. The intensity of it had been agonizing, enthralling, a little frightening. Annie could remember thinking she would shatter—if not for Gavin's arms around her, his voice whispering her name, his sex buried deep inside her.

The memory of that unexpected, unwanted dependency sent the slightest skittering of uneasiness through her.

And yet she refused to regret what she'd done. She hadn't spent the past three years struggling to grow up and take control of her life, only to abdicate responsibility for her actions now.

Besides, Gavin hadn't taken her last night. They'd taken each other. What's more, in this one area at least, their relationship *had* changed. Before, Gavin had dominated their lovemaking. He'd chosen the time and set the pace. He'd been the teacher, she the student. He'd led; she'd followed. He'd been a strong, generous lover who'd always seen to her pleasure, and yet...

And yet, she'd never had the self-confidence to fully express herself, to meet him as an equal.

That certainly wasn't true anymore. In the past dozen hours, she'd expressed herself plenty.

The realization teased at her, suggesting there was an insight, a perception, trembling on the edge of her conscious understanding....

She yawned, and it was gone. It was probably just as well, she decided ruefully, because it was past time for her to get up. She climbed out of bed, wincing as tender inner muscles protested. She found her sleep shirt, shrugged it on, picked up her brush off the dresser and ran it through her hair. She took a deep breath.

Quietly she opened the door.

"Mama!" Sam was up and off the floor in an instant. He shot across the living room and threw himself into her arms, "Sesame Street" and the toy truck he'd been playing with forgotten.

Touched by her son's enthusiastic reception, Annie swept him up and gave him a hug. "Hey, sweetie." She glanced around, noted the laundry basket heaped with clothes sitting on the sofa. She sighed, thinking of the work she hadn't done today—and tried to decide if she were relieved or disappointed that Gavin was nowhere in sight. She returned her attention to Sam. "How're you?"

"'Kay," he said predictably. He patted her cheeks with his hands. "You were atired."

"Yes, I was."

"Dada said 'shh.'" He pressed a pudgy little finger to his lips to demonstrate.

"He did? Well, you were sure quiet. What did you and Dada do today?"

He cocked his head fractionally to one side and considered. "We eated Samcakes and went in the big truck and Dada went splash—" he made an appropriate sound effect "—in big puddles." He frowned all of a sudden, his pale little brows slashing down. "An' Cosmo was a bad, bad, bad doggy. He runned me over and I falled down and cried and gots an owie but it's all better 'cuz Dada gots me Big Bird." Squirming in her arms, he pointed proudly to his left knee, which Annie saw was indeed sporting a Big Bird flexible bandage. "See?"

"Oh, dear," Annie said sympathetically while she tried to sort out what he'd told her. "You fell down?"

"Uh-huh." Sam nodded solemnly. "At the wash-me. Dada said it was a axaboo-boo and kissed it and made it all better."

Kissing things and making them all better seemed to be a *Dada* specialty, Annie thought, as the screen door slammed and Gavin walked into view lugging another overflowing laundry basket.

He stopped dead when he saw her.

Her throat tightened. He looked big and vital in boots and jeans and a dark green T-shirt that clung to his muscled arms and chest. A spattering of raindrops sparkled in his black hair, mixing deliciously with the scent of his after-shave.

Feeling a little awkward as the intimacies of the past twelve hours flashed through her mind, she swallowed and had to force herself to meet his brilliant blue eyes.

"You're up." His voice was low. Husky. With just the faintest note of uncertainty in it. "I was starting to think I was going to have to come in and administer CPR."

She felt a shameless little thrill. For some reason the discovery that he was no more sure of her response than she had been of his was oddly comforting. "I think you already did that."

"Yeah." His gaze flicked from her eyes to her mouth and back again. "I guess I did. I didn't mean to wear you out."

Despite the note of apology in his voice, he couldn't hide the flash of purely male satisfaction that lit his beautiful eyes.

A burst of warmth went through her. Not certain what to say, she tore her gaze away from his too-blue eyes and fixed it on the basket in his hands. She frowned. "There certainly seem to be a lot of pink things in there."

"Yeah." His expression turned sardonic. "That's what happens when somebody leaves a red flannel shirt behind and you wash it with white stuff like T-shirts and socks and underwear."

"Oh, dear."

"Yeah." He walked over and set the basket on the floor next to the other one. "I'm really starting to hate that Laundromat. Did Sam tell you about his accident?" He began folding clothes.

"Yes. He showed me his knee, too." She gave the boy another hug. "Ouch."

"Dada gots a Big Bird, too," Sam said out of the blue. He twisted around and pointed at Gavin's hand. "On his pinger."

Annie looked over and sure enough, there was a colorful strip wrapped around the index finger of Gavin's left hand. "What happened?"

"I slammed it in the dryer," he muttered, flashing her a look that warned her she'd be wise not to comment. He changed the subject. "Your friend Nina called."

"Oh." She supposed she really should stop staring at him.

"She said to remind you her daughter needs to borrow Sam for some Girl Scout thing tonight."

"That's right. Jenny's working on her child-care badge."

"Yeah. She said they'd be by around six to get him."

Annie shifted her gaze to Sam. Here she'd missed seeing him all day, and now he was going to be gone for the better part of the evening. "What do you say, bug? You want to go to Aunt Nee-nee's?" A part of her hoped he'd say no. But even if he only showed a slight hesitation—

"Yes!" Sam nodded enthusiastically, clearly not sharing her concern. But then, going to Nina's was the ultimate treat, since Nina and her kids spoiled him shamelessly.

Gavin cleared his throat. "There are some things we should probably discuss. If it's all right with Nina, if she could keep him a little longer, I thought we could go out, maybe have dinner or something ourselves." Gavin set a stack of pale pink briefs to one side and picked up a pair of Sam's overalls to fold. He looked over at her. "We could pick up Sam on our way home."

Annie hesitated. The prospect of getting dressed up and spending the evening cooped up inside somewhere didn't appeal to her at all.

At the same time, despite last night—or maybe because of it—the idea of being home alone, just her and Gavin, was daunting, as well.

She stood there, debating, when the sun suddenly broke through the clouds outside, flooding the room with light. She glanced out the window and saw that the sky was clearing and that there was every indication it was going to be a nice night.

"Can I pick the place?" she asked slowly.

He shrugged. "Sure. As long as it's not too fancy. I don't own a suit anymore."

"That won't be a problem," she assured him.

And with that, she set Sam on his feet and went to take a shower.

* * *

"Gavin?" Annie said softly.

"What?"

"Are you angry?"

He turned and looked at her in surprise. "No, of course not. Why would you think that?"

"You're awfully quiet. I just thought…maybe you were unhappy about this." *This* was the Rocky Peak Drive-In Theater, where they and several dozen other people in a variety of vehicles were watching Sylvester Stallone and Sharon Stone burn up the silver screen—and each other—in a sexy thriller. "I know it's not what you had in mind."

He turned down the volume on the speaker hanging from the window and looked over at her.

She was slouched on her spine, her bare little feet propped on the dashboard, the picture of relaxation as she sipped an iced cola from a paper cup. Dressed in slim white slacks and an oversize cotton-knit sweater the same pale silvery gold as her hair, she was so beautiful she took his breath away.

"This is fine," he said gruffly. "Really. I guess I'm just a little surprised that you'd rather do this than get all dressed up and go somewhere nice."

"Believe." Her soft voice was wry. "When you work in a restaurant all week, the last thing you want to do on your night off is go to another one."

"I suppose you have a point. But a drive-in?" How come he'd never had a clue she liked them?

She smiled. "Nina got me hooked. We didn't really get to know each other until she and Jerry, husband number three, broke up the summer after Sam was born. We were both on our own without a whole lot of money, and I didn't want to leave Sam any more than I had to. That's when Nina suggested the drive-in. We'd load all the kids into her old station wagon and come for Dollar Night every time the feature changed. It was fun." She sighed.

"There's been talk they may close. I hope not. I really prefer it to the indoor theaters. Here, if the movie is boring you can talk or watch the people in the next car or just stare at the stars and think."

Gavin felt slightly bemused, since the latter was exactly what he'd been doing. "Yeah, I guess so." He stifled a yawn. "One thing is for sure. It certainly would've saved me a bundle, not to mention a sizable amount of time trying to figure out the difference between a *jeté* and a *plié,* if I'd had a clue three years ago that you preferred popcorn with Sly Stallone to lobster bisque and Swan Lake."

Annie was silent a moment. "You could have asked me," she said finally.

"Yeah. Or you could have told me," he countered lazily, angling sideways on the seat so he could stretch his legs. "I'm not too good at ESP. And you don't exactly look like the drive-in type."

He saw her tense and knew he'd misstepped even before he heard the strained note in her voice. "Right."

Not certain what he'd done wrong, much less what to say to make it right, he opted to change the subject. "You know, Nina's not exactly the kind of person I would've thought you'd choose for a friend."

"Nina's terrific," she said immediately.

"I didn't say I didn't like her." Perplexed by her defensiveness, he made sure his tone was mild. "But you've got to admit she's a little . . . flamboyant."

Annie shrugged. "On the outside, perhaps. But underneath she's like everyone else."

"How's that?"

"She's doing the best she can, trying to get by, do right by her kids, find some happiness." She looked over at him, unbending enough to give vent to her curiosity. "What were you two talking about so intently when I walked in after my shower?"

Gavin thought for a second. "That must've been when she was telling me that I'd better be good to you or she'd make me a soprano."

"Oh, no."

It was his turn to shrug. "It was okay." He reached over and clasped her hand, a spark of desire igniting at even that innocent touch. "She had a point, Annie, even though she didn't know it. We didn't use any birth control last night."

She was quiet a moment. "I'm sure it's all right. This— this isn't an optimum time for me to—"

"I wouldn't mind another child," he interrupted, not wanting her to get the wrong idea. "Sam's terrific. You've done a great job with him." In point of fact, that was part of the problem. Their son was such a great kid Gavin couldn't help but regret all that he'd missed—the boy's first breath, first smile, first word, first step. It was almost as bad as knowing he'd missed seeing Annie swollen with his child. Yet he wasn't so far gone that he didn't know they still had too much to resolve without complicating matters that way.

Nor was it his chief concern right now. "That's not why I brought it up. I thought you might be worried about...other things." He glanced at the screen, where Sly wasn't looking worried at all as he ran his hand up Sharon's long, bare leg. "The thing is, I haven't been with anybody since...you."

There was a protracted silence. "Oh," Annie said finally. After another pause, she added, "Why?"

"Why what?"

"Why...not?"

He sighed. Damn. It would be so easy to claim it was because of where he'd been. And yet, he knew he couldn't do it. In this, at the very least, he owed her the truth, after what he'd said that day at Colson. *Annie...you're just a pretty trophy, baby...*

"Because. Nobody else was . . . you."

"Oh," she said in a small voice. "Oh."

As he waited for her to say something more, he suddenly remembered the casual way she'd tossed his flannel shirt on over her underwear that morning more than a month ago. His stomach clenched as he fought a wave of jealousy. He knew his reaction wasn't heroic or admirable or even very fair, not when he'd been the one to end things. For the same reason, he knew she didn't owe him any explanations. But he couldn't help his feelings, dammit.

Still, when she continued to say nothing, he was man enough not to press. He cleared his throat, determined to sound calm and reasonable no matter what it cost him. "The thing is, if you don't want to get pregnant, we probably better figure out what we're going to do from now on."

There was yet another lengthy silence before she ended his misery by saying, "I'll go see the doctor this week."

The spring-loaded coil of tension inside him unwound a notch. Coming on top of the other, he didn't think he could have stood it if she'd banished him back to the couch now. "Good. That's good."

He tugged her closer, maneuvering her until she was sitting in the V of his thighs, her back to his chest. Linking his hands around her waist, he winced as he knocked his elbow against the steering wheel. Yet it did nothing to quell the primitive feelings suddenly coursing through him. Or make him stop wondering if he should mention he'd made a run on the drugstore earlier and was fully prepared to handle certain things . . . now.

He decided not to press his luck.

On the screen, Sly was having no such reservations as he stood on a hotel balcony and kissed Sharon long and passionately, coolly ignoring the huge explosion taking out an entire block of Miami below him.

"Gavin?"

"Hmm?"

"I . . . I don't think I thanked you for letting me sleep today. And for taking care of Sam and the laundry. That was nice."

He nuzzled her hair, enjoying the soft clean scent. "It was no big deal. You work too hard. And your schedule is nuts. I've only done it one day and I'm bushed."

She made a soft sound of protest. "Sam's worth it."

"I'm not debating that. But now that I'm here, you've got some options. You don't have to work nights, waiting tables." He could feel her stiffen. Frustrated, he tried to make her understand that it wasn't her working, per se, that he objected to, but the job itself. "You happen to have some other skills other people don't."

"Like what?" Her tone made it clear she still wasn't happy with the turn the discussion had taken.

"Hell, you've got an art degree. You could take that and work in an art gallery. Part-time—or on commission if you want to set your own schedule. I can understand why it was out of the question before, why you had to have a steady income, but now . . . now that's changed. And if you don't want to do that, you could do something in fashion. You could work in a boutique, or model—"

She turned her head slightly, enough so he could see that the delicate line of her jaw was bunched. "Be a pretty face, you mean? I don't think so." She drew a deep breath. "Despite what you seem to think, waiting tables takes some skill. What's more, I happen to be good at it. Besides, if I left I'd miss Nina and Big Bob and the rest."

He snorted. "I notice you didn't include Clia."

"She's not that bad. She gave me a chance when nobody else would—"

"Aw, come on, Annie."

"And she certainly seems to like you."

He could see they weren't getting anywhere. "Look, just forget I said anything. I don't want to fight, okay? You want to work at the restaurant, that's your choice." *Until I can figure out a way to change your mind.*

She turned to look up at him. "Really?"

"Really." They fell silent and turned their attention back to the movie.

Gavin stroked a circle on the soft skin of Annie's wrist with his thumb, relief thrumming through him when the tension slowly seeped out of her body and she snuggled closer.

"You know," he said quietly, "when you were listing all the good things you could do at the drive-in, you left out the best one."

"I did?" She idly traced her hand over the long muscle that ran lengthwise down the front of his thigh. "What's that?"

He bent his head and pressed a kiss to the silky hollow where her neck and her shoulder met. "Shift around here and I'll show you."

She turned. Their eyes met and his body tightened sharply as he scanned her face. Despite the passage of hours since they'd last made love, she still had the slightly slumberous look of a woman who'd been well and thoroughly satisfied. But now there was a new flush of color in her cheeks and a softly heated look in her big dark eyes that Hollywood couldn't begin to duplicate no matter how hard it tried.

He dipped his head and his mouth closed over hers, hot and hungry. He slid his hand up under her sweater, groaning a little at the feel of her satiny skin against his fingertips.

It was long minutes later before they surfaced for air.

"Gavin?"

"Hmm?"

"I just..." Her breath caught as his hand closed over one satin-covered breast and his thumb began to sweep back and forth across the nipple. She shivered and reached up as soft as a whisper and cupped his cheek in her palm. "There hasn't been anyone else for me, either."

Nine

"Boy, when he's out, he's out," Gavin said softly, cradling Sam's sleep-limp body against his chest as he followed Annie through the darkened house.

She switched on the small lamp on the highboy and continued into Sam's bedroom, amused by the awe in his voice although she fully understood the sentiment.

"There isn't a creature on earth who sleeps as hard as a tired child," she agreed, her quiet voice filled with tenderness as she glanced at Sam's lolling blond head. The toddler hadn't stirred once since they'd picked him up. He'd slept through being taken from the bed he'd been sharing with Steven, Nina's youngest child, to being strapped into his car seat. He'd snored during the entire drive home and hadn't shown a single sign of wakefulness when Gavin had unbuckled him and pulled him out of the truck, nor while being toted into the house.

She pulled back the bed covers and stepped out of the way as Gavin gently lowered the little boy to the mattress. With a contented sigh, Sam rolled to his side. Illuminated by the wedge of light spilling in from the living room, he flung out one soft little arm and burrowed into the pillow, his even breathing never missing a beat.

Annie pulled up the sheet and smoothed his thick straight hair off his forehead, needing the small contact. Staring down at his precious face, she was amazed as she often was by the fierceness of her love for him.

She gave a start as Gavin's arm came around her. "He's pretty damn perfect, isn't he?" he whispered hoarsely.

Surprised by the raw emotion she could hear in his voice, she glanced at him, swamped by an unexpected sense of kinship as she saw many of the same overwhelming feelings she was experiencing reflected in his eyes. "Yes. Yes, he is."

Gavin glanced back at Sam. "Six months ago...I never imagined...I'm glad you went ahead and had him."

She leaned against him, touched by the unexpected admission. "So am I."

They both fell silent, gazing down at the miracle they'd created.

Yet as the moments stretched out, Annie's thoughts slowly shifted from her son to the man at her side. Leaning lightly against his big body, she tried to sort out the tangled web of emotions she was feeling.

There was desire, of course, an ever-present force she could no longer deny. But there was also something more. There was a sense of connection, a fragile new bond that was all the more precious after the bleak years of separation.

Underlying it was a clear new insight, one that had come to her earlier when he'd tossed off that remark about the ballet, about how he didn't have ESP and she should have told him what she liked. Suddenly the thought that had been hovering at the edge of her mind all day had finally jelled.

He was right. She could have told him what she preferred—about that and lots of other things. The power to
be understood had always been in her grasp, but she'd
chosen not to exercise it. All this time she'd condemned
Gavin for not knowing her, for not understanding how she
felt. Yet when it came right down to it, how much effort
had she made to reveal herself?

The answer was: very little. True, she'd been wounded
by her father's view of her, by his insistence on spoiling
her and treating her like a lovely possession. But still . . .

She gave a little shudder as she finally acknowledged
that in some ways—perhaps in the most crucial ones—she
had been a spoiled princess. Hadn't she wasted a good
portion of her life waiting for everyone else to understand her, instead of taking responsibility for herself and
making sure she was understood?

Hadn't she viewed her love for Gavin as a priceless gift
he had no right to question?

And hadn't she considered fighting for his love—and
their marriage—as somehow beneath her?

As much as it shamed her to admit it, the answer to all
those questions was yes.

She swallowed a sigh. At least tonight she'd had the
courage to stand up for herself when he'd dismissed her
job and suggested she model clothes like some pretty doll.
Still, she had a feeling she hadn't done a very good job of
explaining herself. But then, talking about her feelings
remained difficult, particularly when Gavin didn't say
much about his.

Marriage ought to come with a set of directions, she
thought as she stared down at Sam's innocent little face.
Instead, you were sent off with a blank map and left to
find your way day by day. You could hope you'd chosen
the right direction, but you never really knew if you were
headed toward where you wanted to be until you were
there, and it was too late to go back.

And yet she was lucky, she decided, rubbing her cheek lightly against Gavin's big, warm shoulder. She'd been given an unexpected chance to find the right road the second time. And this time—for the first time—it felt as if Gavin was right there beside her.

He yawned. "Come on," he said quietly. He urged her toward the door, which he pulled closed behind him as the clock on the highboy chimed twelve times, marking the official start of a new day.

"Tired?" she said when he yawned again.

"Let's just say I'm more than ready for a full night's sleep. But first, I think we have some unfinished business."

"Such as?"

"Such as this." He reached out, cupped the back of her head in one big hand and gave her a kiss she felt all the way to her toes. He raised his head, and her mouth went dry as she saw the intent, hungry expression on his face.

She pressed a hand to her tender lips. "I thought you were tired."

"I am. But between watching you watch Sly and Sharon and us making out for a full hour in the truck, I'd be... hard-pressed to sleep at the moment. What about you?"

She thought about his startling but deeply gratifying disclosure about his lack of other partners and knew that in this, at least, she had no doubts. "I want you, too." She stepped out of her sandals and took his hand. As simply as that they walked together into her small dark bedroom.

He stopped her inside the doorway. "Annie?"

"What?"

"Switch on the lamp."

She did as he asked, her expression questioning.

With a single step he was at the bed. "I want to see you." He sat and pulled her into the notch of his thighs, his eyes bluer than a Rocky Mountain summer sky. "Among other things . . ." Gently, he threaded his hands through her hair. He pulled her head down and kissed her, long and slow. He teased her with his tongue, tracing the bow of her upper lip, probing the plumpness of the lower one, before he slipped it between her lips and rubbed it against her welcoming one.

She was quivering like a kite in a crosswind when he finally lifted his head. Excitement thrummed through her as he began to undress her, stripping off first her sweater, then her slacks. It intensified as she watched his face grow harder and harder as her clothes fell away and she was left in nothing but a wisp of a pale yellow lace bra and matching thong bikinis that she'd worn with this moment in mind.

He flattened his palm against the gentle curve of her belly. "God, you're pretty."

With a sense of awe, she saw that his hand was trembling.

"But so damn delicate," he continued in a raspy murmur she felt all the way to her toes. "Every time I try to picture you carrying Sam, it just blows me away. . . ."

The wonder in his voice set off a tide of tenderness inside her. "I looked like I'd swallowed a beach ball," she admitted wryly.

A smile tugged at his mouth, but it was bittersweet. He looked up, and the regret she saw in his eyes took her breath away. "I wish I'd been there," he said quietly.

"So do I." It was nothing but the truth.

He unsnapped the front catch of her bra, peeled back the lace cups and replaced them with his hands. "Your breasts are fuller now." He stared at the bounty cupped in his bronzed fingers. "And your nipples have changed. They used to be petal pink. But now they're the color of ripe peaches." He rubbed the tender crests with his fingers, watching avidly as they grew longer and firmer with every stroke. "Did you nurse?"

"The first few months." It was hard to talk when he was touching her this way, and yet there was something decidedly erotic about it, too. "Your son—" she gasped as he pinched her lightly and she felt a light sting of need lower down "—was an utter glutton, too."

"That's my boy." The light words were at odds with the sudden strain in his face. He wrapped his arm around her waist and tipped her back so her breasts were thrust up for him. He made a low, primitive sound deep in his throat as he leaned forward, closed his mouth around one aching tip and began to suckle.

She whimpered, arching her back further. Sensation rippled in a direct line from his heated mouth to the juncture of her thighs. It grew stronger and stronger as he took his time, feasting at first one breast and then the other. She opened her eyes, her throat growing even tighter at the sight of his long, tanned fingers kneading her taut flesh, while his cheeks hollowed with each strong pull of his lips. She reached out and tangled her hand in the cool, inky silk of his hair. When he finally lifted his head, both her breasts were damp and flushed, her nipples were wet and tingling, and the only thing keeping her on her feet was the rock solid prop of his arm.

"Do you like that?" he asked hoarsely.

She trailed her fingers down the side of his face, luxuriating in the feel of his evening whiskers. "You know I do." Her voice was as ragged as his. She leaned forward, pressed her aching breasts against his cotton-covered chest and opened her mouth over his, momentarily the aggressor as she showed him how much.

Gavin groaned, fighting for control as he gently but firmly set her away from him once more. "Annie." Every muscle in his body was hard with the cost of restraint. "Slow down, baby. I want to make this good for you."

"It is," she said breathlessly. "But it would be a thousand times better if you were naked, too."

"In a minute," he promised, knowing that the minute his clothes came off he was going to bury himself inside her. Right now his control was hanging by a thread. All it would take to send him plunging over the edge would be the feel of her hands on his bare flesh.

And he wasn't ready. Not yet.

With a wry twist to his lips at his own stubbornness, he reached out and snagged the edge of her panties. He bent over and slid them down her legs, his control thinning when he brushed his cheek against her taut belly and heard her gasp.

She forgot to breathe altogether a second later as he angled his head and pressed the first of a series of moist, hot kisses to the center of her womanhood.

She clutched at his broad, cotton covered shoulders. After several moments, she said breathlessly, "Gavin?"

"Hmm?" He kissed her again. Only this time he stroked her slick, wet warmth with his tongue.

"If this . . . is a contest—"

She shuddered as he pulled her closer and did it again. A little deeper. A little harder.

"I'm definitely . . . about to . . . win."

The admission sliced through his control like a saber through silk. He'd wanted to go slow. To draw it out, to look his fill, to stroke and taste and feel her. But now . . . he had to be inside her. His body felt hot and aching and explosive with need, and he knew he couldn't wait a second longer.

He surged to his feet, surprising a startled little sound out of her. He yanked down the bed covers, figuring they might as well get between the sheets now, since he didn't intend to get out again anytime in the near future.

He peeled off his clothes in a blur of motion, snatched a condom from his wallet and, with a powerful twist of his body, picked up Annie and lowered her onto the center of the mattress.

His breath hissed out as he followed her down and felt all her soft, silky hills and hollows fit against his own harder, bigger planes and angles.

His breath shivered out again as Annie touched him, restlessly stroking her hands down his back. She clutched at the hard curves of his shoulders and urged him closer. Making a sound that was a combination of frustration and satisfaction as she sobbed for breath, she strained against his weight and rocked her pelvis against his throbbing length.

He braced himself on his hands and lifted himself up, trailing kisses from her lips, to her breasts, to her navel. The clean scent of her warm skin mingled with the faint fragrance of lilacs, making him feel light-headed.

He rocked back on his heels, knelt, fumbled with the foil packet clutched in his hand, ripped it open and rolled the rubber on. A second later he was pressing against her.

"Wait," Annie whispered. "Let me—" She reached for him, making him groan as she wrapped her hand around him. "You feel so good..." She guided him to her, lifting her hips to meet him.

He felt the slippery wet, the incredibly tight softness, as he slowly filled her, inch by aching inch, his gaze riveted on her face. He watched the flush rise across her cheeks, her lips part, her eyes widen on his.

Annie. Look at me. Look at me while I love you, baby. See how perfect we fit together—

The words poured through his mind, but he couldn't say them. Because he was afraid, he realized in a split second of sobering clarity. Afraid she wouldn't say back the words he so desperately needed to hear.

I love you, Gavin. I love you...

And yet he needed to mark her as his own. To lay a claim that no one could dispute.

He began to thrust. He started slowly, drawing out each motion, giving her a chance to adjust to him, wanting to be sure she wasn't feeling any discomfort from their earlier encounters.

His restraint didn't last very long. It began to unravel with her first exultant cry and unwound a little more with the sweep of her hands over the hard curve of his buttocks.

"Yes. Like that. Gavin, please—"

He came completely undone as he realized she was rising to meet each penetration and trying to pull him deeper.

His control vanished. He began to hammer into her, pumping his big body strongly into her smaller, more delicate one. He twined his fingers with hers, bent his head and found her mouth as he felt the pleasure stealing close, gaining on him.

He moved a little faster, drove a little harder, and was rewarded as she began to shudder in the first throes of satisfaction. "Don't stop—" Her entire body bowed up off the bed as she cried out. "Don't stop—don't—"

"It's okay, baby. I've got you." He slid his hands under her derriere and lifted her up. He drove into her one final time. "Oh, Annie, I need you, baby—"

Pleasure slammed into him like a freight train. It stole his breath, blanked his mind, roared right through him and snatched him up for a glorious, wrenching, unparalleled ride.

When it was done, he felt as satisfied as he'd ever felt in his life—and about as substantial as a stick of warm butter. He buried his face in the sweet satiny curve of Annie's shoulder and collapsed. It was long minutes later before he gathered enough strength to roll onto his side.

"Annie." He didn't say anything more.

Her eyelashes fluttered up. Her eyes were heavy, hooded, sated and slumberous, the pupils huge, the thin rim of her irises soft and gleaming. She didn't speak, simply reached out and stroked her fingers lightly over his lips. A tender, languorous smile slowly lit her beautiful face.

Gavin cupped her cheek in his hand, tipped her face to his and kissed her. His mouth was gentle. The kiss was unhurried, melting in its sweetness. He could feel exhaustion creeping through him. He'd had less than five hours sleep in the past thirty-eight hours, and he was definitely beginning to feel the deprivation.

And yet, if he had it to do over again, he wouldn't give up any of those waking hours.

Especially not the past one. Because, as he eased his head back down on the pillow and his gaze met Annie's, he could see in her eyes that she, too, understood that what they'd just shared had been more than a mere physical act, done for pleasure.

It had been an act of hope, a stake in the future, a claiming by them both.

The last thing he saw as he fell asleep was Annie's beautiful, precious face.

And the last thing he thought, as something fierce and primal moved through him, was *You're mine now.*

And this time, I'm going to take good care of you.

Ten

"So, what do you think?" As questions went, it was one of the more stupid ones Gavin had ever asked. All he had to do to know the answer was look across the service porch at Annie's tense face.

She was staring at the washer and dryer he'd bought her as if they were a matched pair of snakes.

"They're very . . . nice," she said carefully.

He knew it was crazy to get bent out of shape over a pair of appliances, but he had to admit her reaction wasn't quite what he'd expected. Excitement, happiness, relief—maybe even a little nod of approval at his thoughtfulness—all would have been perfectly acceptable. Dismay, however, hadn't even been an alternate on his list of possibilities.

"So, what's the problem?" he asked bluntly. "It's not as if I robbed a bank or something. The last time I checked—" try as he might, he couldn't keep the edge out of his voice "—washers and dryers were still legal to own in the state of Colorado. Is it the color? Did you want almond instead of white?''

"White is fine.''

"Then what?'' He watched her purse her pretty lips and wondered why she looked so uncomfortable.

She took a deep breath. "You might have talked to me first. I'd like to be included in these kinds of decisions, Gavin.''

"I explained that,'' he said quickly, not wanting her to think this was like the incident last week, although he still wasn't sure he fully understood what it was she'd been so upset about.

The truth was, he'd thought he was doing something nice when he'd arranged for her to have the night off so he could take her out to dinner. Instead, judging from her reaction, you'd have thought he'd asked her to try her hand at mud wrestling. Still, because of that, and one or two other things that had happened, he now knew she wasn't wild about surprises.

"Listen, this was just one of those unexpected things,'' he told her now. "The distributor who supplies appliances to Gil happened to have these on the truck when he came out to look at the job this morning. He was willing to sell them to me at cost as a professional courtesy. What was I supposed to do? Tell him to forget it? That I had to have my wife's permission?''

"I guess not.''

"Darn it, Annie.'' He took a firm grip on his temper and tried to make her see how unreasonable she was acting. "It's not as if we don't need them. Or as if they're something frivolous, like a diamond tiara or a Rolls Royce. Although—'' he glanced pointedly at the driveway where her Honda was parked next to his truck ''—it's not as if you couldn't use a decent car, too.''

Her exasperation became tinged with alarm. "Don't even think about it,'' she warned. "I like my car.''

"It's not dependable."

"How do you know?"

"The fact that it's going through a quart of oil a week is a pretty good indication." From the look on her face, you'd have thought he'd just said something slanderous about one of her friends, he thought irritably.

"Oh. Well." She lifted her chin stubbornly. "I still like it."

"Right. I suppose you liked the Laundromat, too?"

"As a matter of fact, I did."

"Right," he repeated, his annoyance suddenly taking control of his mouth. "And I suppose going there helped fill all the excess leisure time you have, thanks to your wonderful schedule at the Palomino."

He regretted the heedless words even before she shot him a look that said she thought he was a callous bully.

"Obviously this isn't accomplishing anything," she said in her formal, princess voice. She glanced at her wrist-watch. "And I'm going to be late if I don't get moving, so if you'll excuse me—"

"Aw, come on, Annie—"

It was too late. Like a genie vanishing into a bottle, she disappeared into the house.

"*Shoot!*" He balled his fists in frustration, wanting in the worst way to say something stronger. But he didn't because of Sam, who was out in the yard, playing happily in one of the big cardboard appliance crates.

Besides, he reminded himself, forcing his hands to relax. When it came right down to it, this was no big deal. Every couple disagreed occasionally, and given their history, he and Annie were bound to have more than the normal share of issues to work out.

Still, he had to admit he was vexed. He just didn't get it. What was her problem, anyway? All he was trying to do was make her life a little easier. He didn't understand what there was about that to make her upset.

With a shake of his head, he picked up the vise grip he'd used to tighten the washing machine hose couplings and dropped it in his tool chest. Then he turned the water on and checked for leaks, feeling slightly mollified when the fittings remained dry and tight.

At least something was going right.

He snorted. Okay. So maybe he was overreacting. After all, his relationship with Annie was going well, too, mostly. Today's disagreement was the exception, not the rule. Other than the tension about her job, and the dust-up over dinner, and a few other minor misunderstandings, things were better than he ever could have hoped between them.

Maybe that was why these little disagreements bothered him so much. It frustrated the hell out of him that she stubbornly refused to see that he had some legitimate concerns—her job being a case in point. But when he tried to explain that he worried about her safety being out late at night, or that he hated to see her so tired all the time, it was as if a wall came down.

As far as he could see, the closer together they came about some things, the farther apart they got on others. And, as ridiculous as it appeared when he examined it rationally, he couldn't shake the feeling that each time they argued, he was missing something. Something vitally important.

The thought bothered him. Coming to a sudden decision, he locked his tool chest, checked on Sam and made sure the gate was securely latched, then started toward the house, only to stop when he met Annie coming out.

Poised at the top of the stairs, she looked down at him. Just for an instant the small distance between them seemed enormous.

He didn't like the feeling at all. "Annie, I'm sorry—" He stopped, realizing he didn't really know why he was apologizing.

And then she smiled.

It was slight and tentative, but to Gavin it felt as if the sun had come out after being covered by storm clouds, and all of a sudden whatever it took to put that look on her face seemed perfectly worthwhile. "I didn't mean to upset you," he finished. "I really thought you'd be pleased."

"I know. I'm sorry, too. It's just—"

"Lookee!" Sam's excited voice claimed both their attention. "It's Zoomy Cat! Mama! Dada! Lookee."

Sure enough, the neighbor's oversize Siamese cat stood frozen on the far side of the yard, its bright blue eyes startling in its haughty face, its manner as imperious as a queen. It stared at Sam without blinking for several long seconds, then stalked over and leapt onto the top of the fence, safely out of the little boy's reach.

Sam streaked in the disdainful feline's direction, anyway. "Wanna pet the Zoomy!" he cried. He stopped at the base of the fence and stretched both arms toward the cat, then looked over at Gavin and Annie. "Hep Sam?" he beseeched. "Please?"

Their eyes met, and all the tension melted away. Annie's smile turned teasing. "I bet I know what you're going to get to read tonight."

He shook his head and feigned a groan. "Don't say it. I thought I had him switched to *One Hundred and One Dalmatians*."

She laid her hand on his shoulder. "Hey, it's a tough job but somebody's got to do it."

"Thanks a lot."

She raised her voice. "Sam? You be a good boy for Daddy, and I'll see you in the morning. Okay?"

"Want kitty," he replied.

"I love you, bug."

"Want kitty, please!"

She rolled her eyes. "I've got to go," she told Gavin.

"I know. But not without this." He caught her to him and kissed her, not letting her go until she was shuddering softly against him. "Annie?"

She leaned against him, trying to catch her breath. "What?"

He pressed his car keys into her hand. "Take the truck."

"Alone at last," Nina murmured.

Annie looked up from behind the lunch counter, where the two of them were busy refilling salt shakers and sugar dispensers. She was just in time to see her redheaded friend smile blandly and waggle her fingers at Clia's departing figure.

Nina waited all of half a second for the bell over the door to quit tinkling as the diner's owner exited, then dropped the funnel as if it were a hot potato. "Thank God. I thought she'd never leave. Come on. Let's take a break, have a cup of coffee and a piece of pie to celebrate. My treat."

"You're incorrigible," Annie said with a wry twist to her lips.

"Does that mean you're in?"

Annie took a quick survey of the diner's interior. Things were quiet at the moment. There was a table of teenagers having a postmovie snack, a trio of truck drivers complaining loudly about the new weight limit on one of the mountain passes and a couple in their twenties holding hands and staring soulfully into each other's eyes as their food went unnoticed. She dusted off her hands and reached for the coffee carafe. "Sure. I'll go see how everyone's doing and be right back."

"Great." Nina headed for the lighted pie case along the back wall. "Cherry, chocolate cream or lemon meringue?" she asked over her shoulder.

"Lemon. And milk instead of coffee." She headed around the end of the counter, made a quick circuit of the room, gave the pair of lovers in the corner their bill and rejoined Nina.

With a grateful sigh, she sank onto a stool and propped her feet on the bumper, glad to sit for a minute. Although business had calmed down considerably with the return of more moderate weather, they'd still had a steady stream of customers all evening.

Nina took a large bite of cherry pie. "Yum." She gave an appreciative groan as she chewed and swallowed. "You know—" she pointed her fork at Annie "—this tastes almost as good as you look. Sleeping with The Babe obviously agrees with you. Are you sure both his brothers are married?"

"Yes. Sorry." Annie hadn't told Nina about the change in her and Gavin's relationship. There'd been no need to. Nina had taken one look at Annie's kiss-swollen lips and beard-pinkened cheeks the Saturday she and Jenny had picked up Sam and reached the obvious conclusion.

The redhead sighed. "Bummer." She gazed into her coffee, a wistful expression creeping across her face. "I remember when I used to walk around looking like you." She glanced up, cocked her head, examined Annie and sighed again. "Well, maybe I didn't look *that* good. But I did have a glow on my face." A wicked glint lit her eyes, which were ornamented tonight with alternating bands of shadow in shades of turquoise and lime. "Not to mention whisker burn on my inner thi—"

"Nina!" Annie's protest was softened by a faint laugh. "Be serious."

Nina's smile was unapologetic. "Hon, I am being serious—I am *seriously* jealous. The Man Upstairs never intended for me to be celibate, but it's been two years since Jerry and I split up, and I'm still looking for Mr. Right. Heck—I suppose I'd settle for Mr. Wrong if he was cute enough. And it doesn't help to have you float in every night looking like the cat that ate the canary."

"I don't."

"You do. I'll concede you also look a little tired, but considering the reason why, you're not going to get any sympathy from me."

"I don't believe I asked for any," Annie said mildly. "Besides, being compatible in bed isn't everything."

"Yeah, I suppose that's true." Nina made a mournful face. "Sad, but true." She popped another bite of pie into her mouth, chewed thoughtfully, then said more seriously, "So how're things going, really?"

Annie toyed with the meringue on her pie, carefully flattening the peaks with her fork. "Fine."

Nina waited a few seconds, then prompted patiently, "Is that, 'Life is a box of chocolates and I'm up to my tush in truffles' fine, or 'Beam me up, Scotty, the Klingons are closing fast and I can't find my phaser' fine?"

Annie couldn't help but smile; it was impossible to be too down in the mouth around Nina. "Neither. Just . . . fine fine."

"But?"

Annie looked up. "What?"

"I sense a *but* in there somewhere. What's the matter?"

"Nothing."

The redhead's eyes narrowed. "Right. And I'm old enough to be Brad Pitt's mother."

Annie continued to level the pie topping. "I don't know how to explain it," she said finally.

"So don't. Just tell me what's going on, and I'll figure it out for myself." When Annie remained silent, Nina made an exasperated sound. "I swear, Mrs. Cantrell. I'd rather ask Clia for a raise than try to get personal information out of you. She may be tight with a buck, but with you, it's like trying to pry pearls out of an oyster with a dull toothpick. *Talk.*"

Annie sighed. "Gavin came home early from work today."

"Okay. That explains the glow."

"No. Not today, anyway."

Nina regarded her speculatively. "I take it that means you had a fight?"

"More like a disagreement."

The redhead snorted. "Well, that's certainly normal. About . . . ?" She waited expectantly.

"He bought a washer and dryer."

"And?"

"And what?"

"They're avocado colored? They don't work? They eat your underwear during the spin cycle? What?"

"He didn't talk to me about it first."

Nina widened her eyes. "Oh. Well. No wonder you're unhappy. What despicable thing will the man do next? Force you to accept an unauthorized microwave?"

Annie's expression turned glum. "He did that on Monday." She bit her lip, then admitted, "We also have a new, bigger bed. And he'd get me a different car if I'd let him. And he doesn't like me working here."

"Honey, I hate to break it to you, but having a man want to do nice things for you is good news. And as for this place—well, being a waitress isn't anybody's first career choice."

Annie pushed away her pie. "For heaven's sake, Nina— aren't you proud of what you do?"

The other woman shrugged. "I'm proud I can take care of me and the kids, sure. But the job itself? If I could figure out a way to stay home without going on welfare, or if I had enough education to do something else, I'd be gone in a New York minute." She studied Annie. "That's what I don't get. Why are you resisting the guy so hard?

Ever since I've known you, you've practically killed yourself trying to be a good mom to Sam. Now you've got somebody willing to support you in that effort, and you're not happy about it. I've gotta admit, I just don't get it.''

Annie couldn't believe what she was hearing. "I don't *want* to be supported, Nina. I want to contribute, to be treated like an adult, to be half of a partnership. I guess you'd have to know how I was raised—always being told who I was and what I wanted, rather than being asked—to understand why it's so important to me. But it is.''

"So what does Gavin say when you tell him that?"

Annie shifted uncomfortably. "I haven't...not in so many words. But he has to know—"

"Annie, for heaven's sake! Men don't *know* anything. How do you expect him to understand, if you don't tell him what's going through your head? Lord knows, I'm not the foremost authority, or I wouldn't have struck out so often, but even I know you've gotta be direct. Subtlety is useless. Trust me.''

"But—"

There was a discreet cough. "Excuse me, miss?"

They both looked over to see the infatuated couple were waiting by the cash register to pay their bill.

"I'll get it." Nina climbed to her feet, but not before she leaned over and said, "Trust me. Be blunt with the guy. It's your best chance.''

Annie opened her mouth, then shut it again.

Nina would never fully understand how hard it was for her to open up and talk about her feelings, she realized.

The question was, would Gavin?

"Hey, baby." Gavin caught the screen door and eased it shut behind him as he walked into the sunny kitchen.

Annie looked up from where she was seated at the table. "Hi." Her surprise at seeing him at mid-afternoon on

a weekday was evident in her voice. "What are you doing home?"

"This." He crossed over, bent down and gave her a kiss
that made her glad she was sitting down.

"Well," she said when he finally straightened. She bit
her tingling lips. "That was . . . nice."

"The feeling's mutual." He disappeared into the bathroom to wash his face and hands.

She waited for him to walk back out. "Now. Answer
my question, please?"

He shrugged and set about making a fresh pot of coffee. "One of the guys on the crew fell off the roof this
morning. I ran him to the hospital."

The strain around his eyes suddenly made sense. "Oh,
Gavin. I'm sorry. Is he going to be all right?"

"Yeah. He was lucky. All he broke was his leg. He's
feeling pretty lousy right now, but in a few weeks he
should be as good as new." He turned and lounged back
against the counter, waiting for the coffee to brew.

"What happened?"

His mouth twisted in disgust. "He was horsing around.
I told him a half dozen times to knock it off, but Lee just
isn't real good at listening. He doesn't seem to understand how important being safe on the job is. Or at least
he didn't. Hopefully he does now." He looked around, his
expression brightening slightly. "Where's Samuel, anyway?"

"Still napping."

"Ah." He glanced at his watch. "I guess it is that time.
So why aren't you sleeping, too?"

"Because I need to take care of this." She indicated the
ledger, checkbook and small stack of bills on the table
before her with a rueful grimace. "I'm ashamed to admit
it, but the first of the month came and went last week and
I didn't notice." Her gaze played over him, tracing his
wide shoulders, the firm column of his neck, the sensual

hardness of his lips, and, as usual, her stomach fluttered and her mouth went dry. "I wonder why."

His blue eyes glittered with the unexpected electricity of summer heat lightning. "Keep looking at me like that," he warned in a velvety voice, "and I'll show you."

She gave a soft, rueful laugh and raised her hand as if to hold him off. "Don't you dare. I have to take care of this, or we'll be living in the street. I'm surprised my landlord hasn't called as it is."

Gavin opened the cupboard and reached for a mug. "He did."

"What?"

"Don't worry. I took care of it. *Damn.*" He set the mug on the counter. "That reminds me."

"Gavin—"

"Hang on." To her utter disbelief, he strode over and disappeared out the door.

He was back less than a minute later. "Here." He handed her some papers and walked back to the counter. "I picked those up the day before yesterday and keep forgetting them in the truck." He lifted the glass pot. "You want a cup?"

"No. I do not." Annie dropped the items onto the table without giving them a second glance. "I want to know what you're talking about. Mr. Langley called here? When?"

He took a sip of coffee and considered. "First of the week. Monday—no, Tuesday."

"Why didn't you tell me?"

"You were at work."

"Then afterward?"

"Hell, I don't know. I forgot."

"You *forgot?*"

The muscle in his jaw flexed, but his voice remained even. "That's right."

"But how could you forget something so important—"

"Come on, Annelise. With our schedules I hardly get to see you as it is. I didn't do it on purpose. What's the big deal?"

She stared at him in exasperation. "I need to know these things. I have responsibilities, for heaven's sake!"

"Too darn many if you ask me."

"Gavin—"

"Relax. I told you. I took care of it."

"And what does that mean?" she demanded.

His jaw bunched. "I asked Langley what we owed, he told me, and I sent him a check. No big deal—like I said."

Annie was so stunned by his casual high-handedness she was momentarily speechless. She stared blankly down at the table, trying to gather her thoughts and make some order out of the mishmash of anger and indignation she felt, when her eyes focused on the papers he'd brought. "What are these?"

"Signature cards."

"For what?"

"So you'll be able to sign on my bank accounts."

She took a deep breath. "That's not necessary."

"Sure it is. Legally, it makes good sense. If something happens to me, you'll still have access to any funds. And you might as well be able to just write a check directly for things you need, rather than have me give you the money."

"Why," she said carefully, "would I need you to give me money? I have a job—"

"Which is running you into the ground—"

"And more to the point, we had an agreement." She lifted her chin, growing more formal as she grew increasingly distressed by his failure to understand her feelings. "An agreement about who paid for what—"

"You've got to be kidding." His voice mirrored his astonishment. "For God's sake, Annie. That was before."

The icy grip on her heart tightened immeasurably, making it a struggle to get the next words out. "Before what? Before we started sleeping together?"

His expression darkened. "*No*. Before we started living together as husband and wife, dammit." His eyes narrowed. Suddenly he set down his mug and stalked across the room. So swiftly Annie didn't divine his intent until it was too late, he jerked the chair next to hers away from the table, reached out, grabbed her by the waist and sat back, hauling her sideways onto his lap.

Stunned, she sat motionless for a moment, clutching his shoulders for balance, absorbing his nearness. His denim-clad thighs were rock hard beneath her bottom, the arms wrapped around her midriff as inflexible as steel cables. His scent rose around her, a mix of soap, after-shave and warm male skin, overlaid with a musky hint of perspiration.

She felt a small, sharp, familiar ache of need, and an insidious desire to forget her anger and nestle closer. It made her furious, at herself more than him, not that she had any intention of admitting it. "You're acting like a Neanderthal!"

"That's right. And don't you forget it." He wound a hand in her hair and kissed her.

Annie remained rigid in his arms for all of half a second. Then she succumbed to his heat and hardness and sheer male presence, leaned against him—and nipped him smartly on the lower lip.

"Ouch!" He jerked back and stared at her in astonishment, releasing her hair to rub at the tender spot. "That hurt."

She lifted her chin, choking back the apology that immediately rose to her lips. A part of her, courtesy of the

Brook School for Girls, was appalled by what she'd done. Yet the survivor she'd become was much tougher and insisted it was an act of self-preservation, pure and simple. Another few moments and she would have been as pliant in his hands as a warm lump of Sam's Play-Doh. "I don't appreciate being manhandled. Not when I'm trying to talk to you."

He continued to consider her, and then, amazingly, he let loose a rusty chuckle. "You know, I'm not sure who you are or what you did with my real wife, but I like you." He pursed his lips for a moment. "I apologize," he said formally. He raised an eyebrow. "You want to hit me, too?"

Despite everything, Annie felt a reluctant twinge of amusement. "No."

His mouth lifted, displaying a brief but tantalizing flash of dimples. "Good." He studied her a moment longer, the teasing light in his beautiful eyes gradually fading away. He sighed. "I am what I am, Annie," he said finally. "I don't have a fancy education. I was raised to be about as blue-collar as you can get, and there are certain things that go along with that. You're my wife. I want to take care of you—"

"I can take care of myself," she said firmly. "It's important to me, Gavin. I—I spent enough years as a taker. Now I need to feel like I'm giving back...."

"Baby, you are—"

"But I want to be treated like an equal. Not like some fragile flower you have to look after."

Something flickered in his gaze. His expression tightened and his jaw took on a stubborn cast, only to relax as he took a different tack. "All right, I'll try to do a better job. As long as you'll think about this—does it really matter who pays the rent or buys the food as long as Sam's taken care of? Isn't his welfare what's most important?"

The answer was obvious—and he knew it. "Yes, of course it is. But that doesn't give you the right to take over—"

"I'm not trying to," he insisted, gently tucking a stray strand of hair behind her ear.

His fingers lingered, stroking gently. She felt a familiar sense of resignation, tinged with equal parts frustration and acceptance, as she wondered yet again what it would take for him to understand that she needed to be treated as a full partner in their relationship.

"All I want is to make things better. For all of us." As light as a feather, he slid his fingers down the line of her jaw, then slowly caressed her lips. "That's all." His face tightened once more, but this time it was in a way she recognized. A quiver went through her as she saw the slight flush rise across his cheekbones, the hot and hazy light come into his eyes.

Slowly, his gaze holding hers, he leaned forward.

Annie didn't stop him. On the contrary, she met him halfway, even though she knew this wasn't the answer, that the day was coming when they were going to have to solve their problems in a less pleasurable, more verbal way. And yet...

Their lips met, clung, parted. Their tongues tangled.

Pleasure twisted through her, clear, sharp, sweet. In this, at least, they were perfectly attuned.

He leaned his forehead against hers. "How much longer before Sam wakes up?"

"I don't know. Fifteen or twenty minutes, maybe."

His eyes glinted. "Long enough."

"For what?" she said breathlessly, although she knew perfectly well.

He slid one arm under her knees, the other around her back. "Guess." His eyes blazed as they met hers.

He stood and carried her into the bedroom.

Eleven

———

"Gavin?"

"Hmm?"

"I had a lovely time today. Thank you." Dreamy with contentment, Annie lay on the living room sofa curled spoon fashion against Gavin, her back to his front. The room was dusky, illuminated by the last rays of twilight and the flickering light from the TV set, tuned to a light-hearted spoof that was the Sunday-night movie.

"If I'd known you had a soft spot for the circus as well as drive-in movies, I'd have taken you long ago."

"It was . . . wonderful." The past two weeks had been wonderful, Annie thought. She wasn't quite sure if it was something she'd said or simply that they were finally becoming a real family, but there had been no more misunderstandings about money, no more negative talk about her job, no more surprise purchases or unexpected outings. For once, everything was going smoothly.

He chuckled, the sound rumbling deliciously against her back. "I think the best part was watching Sam's face when he got to pet that elephant. He had the most incredulous look on his face."

Annie smiled, but it was as much a reaction to the easy, relaxed quality of his voice than the recollection itself. "Uh-huh."

He nuzzled her hair, brushing his lips against her temple. "There was only one thing wrong all day."

She twisted her head to look at him, but all she could see was the underside of his jaw. "What's that?"

"I didn't have the chance to do this." He slipped his hand under her T-shirt to cradle her breast and at the same time rose up enough to shift her onto her back beneath him.

She smiled up at him, her gaze warming as she took in the satisfied look on his face. "My. That was slick."

Propped on an elbow, he leaned against the sofa back, the lazy, utterly captivating smile she so rarely saw stealing across his face. "And all this time I bet you thought my high school years were wasted." Holding her gaze, he swept the edge of his thumb back and forth across her nipple.

Desire bloomed in her. Her breasts tightened, straining for his touch, while a familiar tingling ache blossomed between her legs.

In the moment when she could still think, she wondered if it would always be this way between them.

And then she realized it didn't matter. Even if their passion changed in the future from raging wildfire to a steadier, more civilized flame, it would be okay.

She loved that smile and that soft, lazy note in his voice every bit as much as she loved the physical pleasure she found in his arms. She loved hearing him chuckle. She loved the intense blue of his eyes and the little dip in the middle of his top lip. She loved the way his face softened

when he looked at Sam, the sardonic way he had of rais-
ing one slashing black eyebrow, even the way the muscle
in his jaw ticked when he was frustrated about something.

Because she loved . . . him.

The realization took her breath away. For a moment
fear squeezed her heart, as she thought of how badly he'd
hurt her before. And then it was swept away as he slid his
hand out from under her shirt, tried to center his body
over hers and overbalanced, tumbling them both to the
floor.

Saved from having to think, she chuckled with relief as
she found herself sprawled on top of him, her nose
pressed to his chest.

"Sure," he said. "Go ahead and laugh." She lifted her
head, entranced, as he reached up and began to wind a
ribbon of her hair around his long, tanned index finger.
"It's easy to be amused when you land on top."

"Oh, come on," she chided. "I bet the floor isn't nearly
as hard as you are." To prove her point, she rocked slowly
against the rigid warmth of his arousal, which was straining against her belly.

He groaned and reeled her in by her hair.

Annie went willingly, fitting her mouth to his, feeling
warm and fuzzy and more than a little drunk on desire.
Taking control of the kiss, she broached the barrier of his
teeth with her tongue. She took her time and explored
him, tasting, touching, stroking. He stroked her back,
running his big hands under her shorts to cup her bottom, and she whimpered, making soft little sounds of
satisfaction.

By the time she lifted her head, the strong angles of his
face were standing out sharply, flushed from the need
clearly riding him.

"Come on." He sat up, powerful enough to lift her with
him, pushed her to her feet and stood himself. He urged

her toward the bedroom. "I don't want to worry about Sam waking up and finding us buck naked on the rug."

She tried to look demure. "Are we about to be buck naked?"

"Absolutely. I want to be inside you."

The flat declaration of intent sent a shiver of excitement through her. So did the look in his eyes as he shut the bedroom door, enveloping them in the dusky shadows of the little room. He yanked his T-shirt over his head and peeled out of his shorts, then helped her to do the same.

Clothed in nothing but the dim silvery light, they faced each other. She caught her breath, awed as she always was by his sheer physical perfection, excited by the heated way he looked at her in turn.

"Annie." The low, raspy sound of his voice made her shiver. So did his next words. "Touch me..."

"Where?"

"Anywhere. Everywhere..."

He didn't have to ask her twice. She stepped forward. Going up on tiptoe, she gripped the velvety curves of his biceps for balance and began to kiss him, starting at the underside of his jaw, trailing her mouth down the side of his neck to the strong notch where his collarbones met. As her mouth moved down to find the tiny beaded points of his nipples, her hands crept up. She traced the firm line of his shoulders and the smooth column of his neck before she swept her hands down, over his lean sides and narrow hips to cup his muscled buttocks. And all the while, she gently circled her hips, brushing the satiny curve of her lower abdomen against him.

He groaned. "Annie. Touch me..."

"Here?" She squeezed the taut curves of his ridiculously little backside in her hands.

He quivered like a stallion being teased by a mare. "No."

"Here?" She released him, sank back on her heels and unhurriedly trailed her fingers along the downy stripe of hair on his belly.

"No." The word came from between clenched teeth.

"How about here?" She traced a fingertip over his hot male length, rubbed the broad tip and raked her fingers through the surrounding cloud of jet black hair.

"Annie—"

"Shh. I know." With deliberate slowness, she measured his hardness in her hands and finally began to stroke him, feeling shy and bold and brazen and audacious all at the same time.

"Yes. Oh, baby, *yes—*"

"What about here?" Without letting go of him, she found his hand and pressed it to the needy place at the top of her own thighs, moaning as he gently probed her wet softness, irrefutable evidence of her own state of readiness.

Slowly he slid his fingers over her until her control blew away like chaff on the breeze. "Oh. Gavin. Please."

"Yes."

They toppled onto the bed together. He rolled over her, settling heavily between her thighs, the ridged hardness of his belly pressing her down before he plunged forward. She arched up to meet him, and he made a deep guttural sound as she sheathed him in her slick, tight warmth.

Annie cried out, too. She could feel him deep inside her, could feel the incredible heat and pressure. She moved, rising to meet him, wanting all of him, welcoming each long thrust as he set a quick, demanding pace. She felt as if she were burning up inside, a sensation that got hotter and bigger with each deep, driving motion of his big body until pleasure exploded inside her. Her back bowed. Above her, Gavin went rigid and made a strangled, primal sound deep in his throat as the milking motions of her body triggered his own flooding release.

Annie collapsed, then gave a mew of surprise as he unexpectedly gripped her tightly and rolled them so he was beneath her. She rubbed her cheek against his warm, solid chest, her heart pounding like a trip-hammer. "That didn't take very long."

He chuckled. "Sorry. That's what happens when you torture a guy first."

"I wasn't complaining."

"Neither was I."

She smiled. Draped limply across his chest, she felt pleasantly sleepy, but she couldn't quit touching him. She stroked his cheek and touched her fingers to his mouth, her own curving with happiness when she felt him purse his lips in a tiny kiss. She explored the varying textures of the whiskers at different locations on his face and sifted her hands through his silky dark hair. She couldn't remember a time when she'd ever felt so happy.

Eventually Gavin shifted. "Annie?"

"Hmm?" With a start, she realized she must have drifted off. She opened her eyes and found the room was velvet dark.

"There's something I need to talk to you about."

She nestled closer, frowning at the faint note of strain she could hear in his voice. It was out of place, an unwanted pebble dropped into the serene pool of her contentment. She yawned. "Now?"

"Yeah. Shift over so I can turn on the light."

Feeling boneless, she nonetheless did as he requested, rolling onto her side. She felt him stretch, then blinked when the bedside lamp came on. Slowly her eyes adjusted. She watched as he bunched a pillow behind his back and sat up. An uneasy tickle crept down her spine as she saw his serious expression. "What is it?"

He took a moment as if to gather his thoughts. "It's about my job. Once the Ebersole house is finished, I'm going to be out of work."

"Oh, Gavin." Surprised and dismayed, she sat up, feeling an immediate well of sympathy. She knew how much he liked his job. "I'm sorry. What happened?" Instinctively she drew the sheet up to her breasts, her modesty so ingrained it was second nature.

"Gil's moving his operation. He's signed a contract with a land developer to build spec houses in a brand-new subdivision. He asked me to sign on as his foreman, but I told him I didn't see how I could do it."

Perplexed, she studied him. "But why? I thought you liked working for him."

"I do."

"Then is it the job itself? Is there some problem—"

"No, that's not it. I'd have more responsibility. And it would mean longer hours, less time at home, at least at first. But the pay is good, and it's a great opportunity—hell, it's the kind of job I thought would never come my way again after what happened in Pueblo." His voice took on an undeniable edge of regret. "Plus, Gil could really use my experience. This is going to be a big change—and a big risk—for him. After everything he's done, helping me get the truck, giving me a job, believing in me, it'd be a chance to pay him back a little, to be there for him for a change."

It sounded tailor-made for him, Annie thought. He was too smart, too energetic and had too much organizational talent to be happy for long as a simple carpenter. She tried to figure out what she'd missed. "Why not do it, then?"

He shoved a hand in his hair, raking an errant lock off his forehead. "The subdivision happens to be in Billings."

"Billings?" she said blankly.

He nodded, his eyes riveted to her face. "Montana."

"Oh. Oh, dear."

"Yeah. Exactly. That's why I turned Gil down. I know it may have taken me a while, but I know how much being here means to you, Annie, how much you care about this house and your friends—and even your job. I explained all that to Gil."

She stared at him, suddenly feeling dizzy. "Wait a minute. You turned him down because of... me?"

"Well... yeah."

"Without asking me what I thought?"

"Are you telling me I was wrong?" His look of surprise and sudden hope would have been touching if it hadn't been so totally infuriating. "You mean you think I should take it?"

She shot him a disbelieving stare. "*No*, you—you jackass." She scrambled off the bed, snatched a T-shirt off the floor and yanked it on, too agitated to care that it was his. She jerked her hair free of the collar and tossed it over her shoulders. "I mean, you should have spoken to me." She marched over and flung open the door.

"Hey, wait a minute!" He lunged off the bed, grabbed his shorts and hauled them on. "Where do you think you're going? We're not done talking—"

"Done?" She tossed the word over her shoulder. She headed toward the kitchen, not because she needed anything but because she didn't know where else to go. "You can't be done with something you never started in the first place, Gavin! I may not know much, but I do know that."

He caught up with her when she was barely halfway to the archway. "I don't know what the hell you're so mad about! I was only trying to do what I thought was best—" He clamped a hand on her shoulder.

She shook him off and whirled. "Oh, really? For who? For me? Don't be insulting! This isn't about my best interest. This is about your need to be in control."

"*My* need to be in control? You're the one who has to have her finger on everything. I can't pay a bill or buy a box of cereal or express a concern without you jumping all over me.''

"Well, at least you get a chance to say something. I'm not even told what's going on so that I can *have* an opinion!''

"Oh, that's rich. Everything I've done has been to help—''

"Really?'' Her voice rose shrilly. "I suppose the next thing you're going to say is that you were only thinking of me when you claimed things were over between us three years ago!'' For the life of her, she didn't know where the furious words came from, but suddenly there they were.

His expression darkened ominously. "As a matter of fact, I was!''

"And how was that, Gavin? I loved you and you tossed me aside—''

"Yeah? Well you sure as hell had a strange way of showing your devotion, Annie! I don't remember you saying a word—not a word—of protest when I cut you loose. You sat there as cold as an ice princess, and you were out the door before I finished the last damn sentence!''

"Oh! How dare you—''

"How dare you not stand by me!'' he shouted, only to break off when her eyes went wide with dismay as her gaze fixed on a spot behind him.

He spun around and came face-to-face with Sam. *"Godalmighty."*

The little boy stared up as if Gavin were some stranger, his bright blue eyes huge in his little face, his bottom lip quivering. "W-want M-mama,'' he whispered tremulously.

"Sam.'' Although Gavin tried to temper his voice, it still sounded rough and ragged. "It's okay. Come here, son—'' He reached for the boy.

"No!" With a shrill cry, Sam darted around him and launched himself at Annie. "Want Mama!" He wrapped both dimpled arms around her knees, hid his face against her legs and burst into tears.

Except for the muffled sound of the little boy's sobs and the background murmur from the television, the sudden silence in the room was deafening.

And then Gavin made a choked-off cry of his own, stalked over and slapped off the TV set. His gait jerky, he continued on to the window where he braced his hands against the frame and stood, head bowed, shoulders weighted down.

His action jolted Annie out of her paralysis.

Feeling as if her heart were breaking, she picked Sam up and cuddled him against her. "Shh, sweetie. It's all right. Really." She rocked him in her arms, murmuring a steady stream of reassurances. "It's all right, bug. There's nothing to be afraid of. Mama's here." She rubbed her cheek against the top of his head and stroked her hand up and down his back, her voice thick with misery despite her comforting words.

But she didn't cry.

Because there were some hurts that were beyond the reach of tears. And—she gave Sam another reassuring pat—some needs that had to come first.

Just as there were some things that had to be said. No matter how scared or reluctant or awkward she felt. Or how terrified she was that she'd say the wrong thing and it would send Gavin away forever.

Because, as she looked across the room at the defeated line of his back, she finally understood that if she remained silent this time, she was going to lose him anyway.

In her arms Sam gave one last little shudder, hiccuped and sagged against her, falling silent.

She couldn't put it off any longer. "You were right, Gavin."

"About what?" His voice was low and scratchy, tinged with an unfamiliar trace of bitterness.

She continued to rock, choking back her fear, taking comfort in the feel of Sam's silky head against her cheek. "I didn't fight for our marriage. I loved you so much, but I was afraid."

"What?" Slowly he turned.

"I was eight when my mother died, and Daddy sent me away. All my life I wanted him to see me as a real person, instead of as a pretty possession. Then he died and I—I had to face that it was never going to happen.

"But I told myself it was okay, because I had you. It didn't matter that we hadn't known each other very long, or that we never seemed to talk about how we felt. I was so in love with you. I thought that was enough. I thought we could get through anything."

"Annie—"

"And then...when all the trouble started, you shut me out completely except in bed. I didn't know why, so I started to think you blamed me."

Gavin's insides cartwheeled. "For what?" He took a step toward her and stopped, trying to make sense of what she was saying.

Her eyes were focused inward on something only she could see. "I thought you'd kept silent to protect me."

"No." He shook his head. "No. I did it for Max. He'd been my friend, my mentor—I didn't want him to have done what he did. And I did it for myself, because I was arrogant enough to think I could handle it on my own. And then, when it all went south, when the building went down and Russert was hurt, I realized I had nobody to blame but myself. I was angry at Max, at the situation, at the D.A., but I was angriest at myself."

"But why didn't you tell me?"

He sighed. "Ego, I guess. I felt guilty enough that I'd misjudged things. And I thought you believed I'd been in on it from the beginning. Looking back, it seems crazy that it should have mattered, but it did."

She echoed his sigh. "I think we were both a little crazy by then. I know I was, particularly when I began to suspect I was pregnant. I was so afraid. But I clung to the idea that if I just didn't lose faith, our love would see us through. And then I came to tell you the news, but before I could, you told me you didn't love me, that I'd just been a trophy of your success. It was my worst nightmare come true. Someone I loved was sending me away. Because I wasn't the kind of person they could love." She swallowed and met his gaze, the remembered hurt stark in her eyes for him to see. "I felt like such a fool. I was so ashamed, so mortified—because it didn't matter. All I could think was I had to escape before you realized how desperately I still loved you—"

Her voice broke, and the soft sound shattered the last barrier around his heart.

"Oh, baby." He was across the room without knowing how he got there. "Don't—" He reached for her, his hands shaking.

She took a step back. "No. Please. I need—I need to finish this. After Sam came, I told myself I'd changed. That I'd grown up, taken charge of my life. I told myself I was happy. And then you showed up, and even though I wouldn't admit it, not even to myself, somewhere inside I knew I'd never stopped loving you. That was really why I never divorced you. And it scared me. So I told myself you were like Daddy. That you were just a controller, interested in having your way no matter what. But you're not, Gavin. I know that. You're good and you're decent and you're honest. You're a wonderful father. And I love you so much—but it's not enough. I need to feel that I have something to contribute. To know that I'm more than a pretty face—"

He couldn't stay silent a moment longer. "Oh, baby, you are. Don't you understand? That day at Colson, I was angry, but *I* was afraid, too. I was afraid you wouldn't wait for me. And I was even more afraid you would, and that I'd come out of jail as something less than a man and—and I couldn't stand the thought. Even worse, in some ways, I *was* like Max when it came to you. I saw the pretty face, the fancy schools, the society life-style—and I loved the image, too. Except it was never the real you, was it?"

She shook her head, her eyes bright with tears.

He reached out and cupped her cheek with his hand. "I know that now, Annie. Because the woman I love is the person you've become. The woman who struck out on her own, who nurtured and safeguarded our son. Who knows the value of honest labor and who chooses her friends for their hearts, not their hair color. Who's not afraid to stand up to me—or to stand alone if she has to. Only I hope you don't want to, Annie." He swallowed against the sudden lump in his throat and gently touched his thumb to her lips. "Because I need you. I'm not whole without you. We fit together perfectly, baby—and I love you. I love you so much."

"Oh, Gavin," she whispered. "I love you, too."

Unable to stand the idea of being apart from her even one second longer, he took the last step forward and encircled her in his arms. His mouth met hers, and her lips were soft and yielding and as sweet as summertime, and he knew he'd been right the day he'd seen her in the grocery store.

She was a woman who could haunt a man's days and bedevil his nights, who could ruin him for anyone else.

She was a woman to cherish.

She was also somebody's mother—a reality Gavin was sharply reminded of as a pointy little elbow poked him in the ribs. With a good-natured sigh, he released her soft lips, lifted his head and glanced down.

Bright blue eyes, the same shade as his own, peered up at him as Sam stirred in Annie's arms. "Hey, Samuel." He felt a slight edge of apprehension as he recalled the child's earlier distress. "You feeling better?"

The little boy yawned, looked from Annie to Gavin, then smiled and held out his arms to his father. "Uh-huh. Sam is *oh*-kay."

Overcome with tenderness, Gavin gathered him close and looked at Annie. "Me, too," he said softly. "Me, too."

Annie walked slowly into the living room of her little house, her footsteps echoing as she took one last look around.

Sunshine striped the faded floor and played on the bare white walls. Stripped of furniture and familiar objects, the place looked slightly shabby. Yet Annie knew she would always remember it as warm and welcoming and special. It was here that Sam had smiled his first smile, said his first word, taken his first step. It was here that she'd found herself and learned the value of self-respect. It was here she'd discovered that love was worth fighting for—and found the courage to do just that.

"Annie?"

She turned as the screen door twanged.

Gavin stood framed in the doorway, his handsome face worried. "Are you all right, baby?"

"Yes. I'm just having one last look around."

He let the screen door slap shut and came to stand beside her. "You're not feeling queasy again, are you?"

"No." She gave a soft sigh of pleasure as his arm came around her. "I'm fine."

"Good—because you're the only one who is. Sam says he's hungry, and Nina just came by to remind me, again, that she and the kids are coming for Thanksgiving." He snorted. "As if I'd forget." He shook his head. "At this rate, we're not going to make it out of the driveway today, much less make Billings."

She would tell him her news later, she decided. Tonight. After they got Sam tucked into bed. After they made love to celebrate their new life together.

Then would be the perfect time to tell him he was going to be a father again.

"Annie." He slid his hand down her arm and gently turned her to face him. "Are you sure you want to go?"

She met his brilliant blue gaze and thought how much she loved him. "Yes. Absolutely."

His smile stole her breath. "Okay, then."

Hand in hand, they turned and started toward their future.

*   *   *   *   *

The first book in the exciting new
Fortune's Children series is
HIRED HUSBAND
by *New York Times* bestselling writer
Rebecca Brandewyne

Beginning in July 1996
Only from Silhouette Books

Here's an exciting sneak preview....

Minneapolis, Minnesota

As Caroline Fortune wheeled her dark blue Volvo into the underground parking lot of the towering, glass-and-steel structure that housed the global headquarters of Fortune Cosmetics, she glanced anxiously at her gold Piaget wristwatch. An accident on the snowy freeway had caused rush-hour traffic to be a nightmare this morning. As a result, she was running late for her 9:00 a.m. meeting—and if there was one thing her grandmother, Kate Winfield Fortune, simply couldn't abide, it was slack, unprofessional behavior on the job. And lateness was the sign of a sloppy, disorganized schedule.

Involuntarily, Caroline shuddered at the thought of her grandmother's infamous wrath being unleashed upon her. The stern rebuke would be precise, apropos, scathing and delivered with coolly raised, condemnatory eyebrows and in icy tones of haughty grandeur that had in the past reduced many an executive—even the male ones—at Fortune Cosmetics not only to obsequious apologies, but even to tears. Caroline had seen it happen on more than one occasion, although, much to her gratitude and relief, she herself was seldom a target of her grandmother's anger. And she wouldn't be this morning, either, not if she could help it. That would be a disastrous way to start out the new year.

Grabbing her Louis Vuitton tote bag and her black leather portfolio from the front passenger seat, Caroline stepped gracefully from the Volvo and slammed the door. The heels of her Maud Frizon pumps clicked briskly on the concrete floor as she hurried toward the bank of elevators that would take her up into the skyscraper owned by her family. As the elevator doors slid open, she rushed down the long, plushly carpeted corridors of one of the hushed upper floors toward the conference room.

By now Caroline had her portfolio open and was leafing through it as she hastened along, reviewing her notes she had prepared for her presentation. So she didn't see Dr. Nicolai Valkov until she literally ran right into him. Like her, he had his head bent over his own portfolio, not watching where he was going. As the two of them collided, both their portfolios and the papers inside went flying. At the unexpected impact, Caroline lost her balance, stumbled, and would have fallen had not Nick's strong, sure hands abruptly shot out, grabbing hold of her and pulling her to him to steady her. She gasped, startled and stricken, as she came up hard against his broad chest, lean hips and corded thighs, her face just inches from his own—as though they were lovers about to kiss.

Caroline had never been so close to Nick Valkov before, and, in that instant, she was acutely aware of him—not just as a fellow employee of Fortune Cosmetics but also as a man. Of how tall and ruggedly handsome he was, dressed in an elegant, pin-striped black suit cut in the European fashion, a crisp white shirt, a foulard tie and a pair of Cole Haan loafers. Of how dark his thick, glossy hair and his deep-set eyes framed by raven-wing brows were—so dark that they were almost black, despite the bright, fluorescent lights that blazed overhead. Of the whiteness of his straight teeth against his bronzed skin as a brazen, mocking grin slowly curved his wide, sensual mouth.

"Actually, I *was* hoping for a sweet roll this morning—but I daresay you would prove even tastier, Ms. Fortune," Nick drawled impertinently, his low, silky voice tinged with a faint accent born of the fact that Russian, not English, was his native language.

At his words, Caroline flushed painfully, embarrassed and annoyed. If there was one person she always attempted to avoid at Fortune Cosmetics, it was Nick Valkov. Following the breakup of the Soviet Union, he had emigrated to the United States, where her grandmother had hired him to direct the company's research and development department. Since that time, Nick had constantly demonstrated marked, traditional, Old World tendencies that had led Caroline to believe he not only had no use for equal rights but also would actually have been more than happy to turn back the clock several centuries where females were concerned. She thought his remark was typical of his attitude toward women: insolent, arrogant and domineering. Really, the man was simply insufferable!

Caroline couldn't imagine what had ever prompted her grandmother to hire him—and at a highly generous salary, too—except that Nick Valkov was considered one of the foremost chemists anywhere on the planet. Deep down inside Caroline knew that no matter how he behaved, Fortune Cosmetics was extremely lucky to have him. Still, that didn't give him the right to manhandle and insult her!

"I assure you that you would find me more bitter than a cup of the strongest black coffee, Dr. Valkov," she insisted, attempting without success to free her trembling body from his steely grip, while he continued to hold her so near that she could feel his heart beating steadily in his chest—and knew he must be equally able to feel the erratic hammering of her own.

"Oh, I'm willing to wager there's more sugar and cream to you than you let on, Ms. Fortune." To her utter mortification and outrage, she felt one of Nick's hands slide insidiously up her back and nape to her luxuriant mass of sable hair, done up in a stylish French twist.

"You know so much about fashion," he murmured, eyeing her assessingly, pointedly ignoring her indignation and efforts to escape from him. "So why do you always wear your hair like this...so tightly wrapped and severe? I've never seen it down. Still, that's the way it needs to be worn, you know...soft, loose, tangled about your face. As it is, your hair fairly cries out for a man to take the pins from it, so he can see how long it is. Does it fall past your shoulders?" He quirked one eyebrow inquisitively, a mocking half smile still twisting his lips, letting her know he was enjoying her obvious discomfiture. "You aren't going to tell me, are you? What a pity. Because my guess is that it does—and I'd like to know if I'm right. And these glasses." He indicated the large, square, tortoiseshell frames perched on her slender, classic nose. "I think you use them to hide behind more than you do to see. I'll bet you don't actually even need them at all."

Caroline felt the blush that had yet to leave her cheeks deepen, its heat seeming to spread throughout her entire quivering body. Damn the man! Why must he be so infuriatingly perceptive?

Because everything that Nick suspected was true.

* * * * *

To read more, don't miss
HIRED HUSBAND
by Rebecca Brandewyne,
Book One in the new
FORTUNE'S CHILDREN series,
beginning this month and available only from
Silhouette Books!

This exciting new cross-line continuity series unites
five of your favorite authors as they weave five
connected novels about love, marriage—and
Daddy's unexpected need for a baby carriage!

Get ready for

THE BABY NOTION by Dixie Browning (SD#1011, 7/96)
Single gal Priscilla Barrington would do anything for a
baby—even visit the local sperm bank. Until cowboy
Jake Spencer set out to convince her to have a family
the natural—and much more exciting—way!

And the romance in New Hope, Texas, continues with:

BABY IN A BASKET
by Helen R. Myers (SR#1169, 8/96)

MARRIED...WITH TWINS!
by Jennifer Mikels (SSE#1054, 9/96)

HOW TO HOOK A HUSBAND (AND A BABY)
by Carolyn Zane (YT#29, 10/96)

DISCOVERED: DADDY
by Marilyn Pappano (IM#746, 11/96)

DADDY KNOWS LAST arrives in July...only from

DKL-D

MILLION DOLLAR SWEEPSTAKES

FORTUNE'S Children™

New York Times Bestselling Author
REBECCA BRANDEWYNE

Launches a new twelve-book series—FORTUNE'S CHILDREN
beginning in July 1996 with Book One

Hired Husband

Caroline Fortune knew her marriage to Nick Valkov was in
name only. She would help save the family business, Nick
would get a green card, and a paper marriage would suit both
of them. Until Caroline could no longer deny the feelings Nick
stirred in her and the practical union turned passionate.

MEET THE FORTUNES—a family whose legacy is greater than
riches. Because where there's a will…there's a wedding!

Look for Book Two, *The Millionaire and the Cowgirl*,
by Lisa Jackson. Available in August 1996 wherever Silhouette
books are sold.

Silhouette's recipe for a sizzling summer:

* Take the best-looking cowboy in South Dakota
* Mix in a brilliant bachelor
* Add a sexy, mysterious sheikh
* Combine their stories into one collection and you've got one sensational super-hot read!

Summer Sizzlers

MEN OF *Summer*

Three short stories by these favorite authors:

Kathleen Eagle
Joan Hohl
Barbara Faith

Available this July wherever Silhouette books are sold.

Look us up on-line at: http://www.romance.net

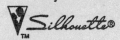

Available in July from

V SILHOUETTE YOURS TRULY™

THE CASE OF THE LADY IN APARTMENT 308
by Lass Small

Ed Hollingsworth's observations about the lady in apartment 308: great figure, nice smile when she does smile, strange friends, kooky habits. His first thought had been *eviction* but now Ed's hoping to take his investigation directly behind sexy Marcia Phillips's closed door....

WHEN MAC MET HAILEY
by Celeste Hamilton

Hailey on Mac: He's cute, a great kisser...but a single dad! I've already been down that road before.... *Mac on Hailey:* My friends think I should date someone nice, maybe find a mom for my young daughter. The one hot number I keep coming back to is Hailey's....

∽∾∽∾∽∾∽∾∽∾∽∾

Love—when you least expect it!

YT796

SILHOUETTE... Where Passion Lives

Add these Silhouette favorites to your collection today!
Now you can receive a discount by ordering two or more titles!

SD#05819	WILD MIDNIGHT by Ann Major	$2.99	☐
SD#05878	THE UNFORGIVING BRIDE	$2.99 U.S.	☐
	by Joan Johnston	$3.50 CAN.	☐
IM#07568	MIRANDA'S VIKING by Maggie Shayne	$3.50	☐
SSE#09896	SWEETBRIAR SUMMIT	$3.50 U.S.	☐
	by Christine Rimmer	$3.99 CAN.	☐
SSE#09944	A ROSE AND A WEDDING VOW	$3.75 U.S.	☐
	by Andrea Edwards	$4.25 CAN.	☐
SR#19002	A FATHER'S PROMISE	$2.75	☐
	by Helen R. Myers		

(limited quantities available on certain titles)

TOTAL AMOUNT	$_____
DEDUCT: 10% DISCOUNT FOR 2+ BOOKS	$_____
POSTAGE & HANDLING	$_____
($1.00 for one book, 50¢ for each additional)	
APPLICABLE TAXES**	$_____
TOTAL PAYABLE	$_____
(check or money order—please do not send cash)	

To order, send the completed form with your name, address, zip or postal code, along with a check or money order for the total above, payable to Silhouette Books, to: **In the U.S.:** 3010 Walden Avenue, P.O. Box 9077, Buffalo, NY 14269-9077; **In Canada:** P.O. Box 636, Fort Erie, Ontario, L2A 5X3.

Name:_____

Address:_____ City:_____

State/Prov.:_____ Zip/Postal Code:_____

**New York residents remit applicable sales taxes.
Canadian residents remit applicable GST and provincial taxes.

Silhouette®
TM

SBACK-JA2

You're About to Become a

Privileged Woman

Reap the rewards of fabulous free gifts and benefits with proofs-of-purchase from Silhouette and Harlequin books

Pages & Privileges™

It's our way of thanking you for buying our books at your favorite retail stores.

PROOF OF PURCHASE
SD-PP156
Offer expires October 31, 1996

Harlequin and Silhouette— the most privileged readers in the world!

For more information about Harlequin and Silhouette's PAGES & PRIVILEGES program call the Pages & Privileges Benefits Desk: 1-503-794-2499

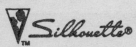

Silhouette®

SD-PP156